ON THE LANDING

ON THE LANDING

STORIES

BY

YENTA MASH

TRANSLATED BY ELLEN CASSEDY

WITH AN AFTERWORD CO-AUTHORED BY JESSICA KIRZANE

A YIDDISH BOOK CENTER TRANSLATION

NIU Press / DeKalb IL

Northern Illinois University Press, DeKalb 60115
© 2018 by Ellen Cassedy
All rights reserved

27 26 25 24 23 22 21 20 19 18   1 2 3 4 5
978-0-87580-793-5 (paper)
978-1-60909-249-8 (e-book)
Book and cover design by Yuni Dorr

This is a work of fiction. All characters are products of the author's imagination, and any resemblance to persons living or dead is entirely coincidental.

The stories "The Bridegroom Tree," "Resting Place," "Bread," "Alone," "The Payback," and "On the Landing" were originally published in Yiddish in *Tif in der tayge* [Deep in the Taiga] (Tel Aviv: Farlag Yisroel Bukh, 1990), and have been translated with the kind permission of Regina Novak.

The stories "Mona Bubbe," "The Irony of Fate," "The Cap," "Ingathering of Exiles," and "Retirees" were originally published in Yiddish in *Meshane mokem* [A Change of Place] (Tel Aviv: Farlag I. L. Peretz, 1993), and have been translated with the kind permission of Regina Novak.

The stories "By the Light of the Moon" and "The Second Time Around" were originally published in Yiddish in *Besaraber motivn* [Bessarabian Themes] (Tel Aviv: Farlag I. L. Peretz, 1998), and have been translated with the kind permission of Regina Novak.

The stories "A Seder in the Taiga," "At the Western Wall," and "Erika" were originally published in Yiddish in *Mit der letster hakofe* [The Last Time Around] (Tel Aviv: H. Leyvik Farlag, 2007), and have been translated with the kind permission of H. Leyvik Publishing House.

The following stories appeared previously in English translation by Ellen Cassedy: "Resting Place" in *B O D Y*, December 2016; "The Payback" in *PEN America*, July 2016; "A Seder in the Taiga" in *Pakn Treger*, Spring 2017; "On the Landing" in *Pakn Treger*, Spring 2016; "By the Light of the Moon" in *Tiferet*, Autumn 2017; "Mona Bubbe" in *Have I Got a Story for You: More Than a Century of Fiction from the* Forward, Ezra Glinter, ed. (New York: W. W. Norton & Company, 2016); "Ingathering of Exiles" in *Words Without Borders*, Fall 2016; "The Second Time Around" in *JewishFiction.net*, no. 19, September 2017.

Library of Congress Cataloging-in-Publication Data is available online at
http://catalog.loc.gov

Contents

ON THE LANDING

THE BRIDEGROOM TREE

> On the road stands a tree
> Bowed down to the ground
> All the birds have flown away
> There's not a bird around
> —Itsik Manger

Our Bessarabia used to be known far and wide for its roads. They say every cripple has his own unique deformity, and in the same way our roads were one of a kind, unlike those of any other region. They were an abomination.

We were located at the southern tip of the Great Russian Empire, pressed up against Romania, which stubbornly insisted on being called "Greater Romania," and squeezed between two rivers with Biblical-sounding names, the Prut and the Dniester. Our region was the eternal scapegoat, always handy for redeeming sins and settling disputes between neighbors. We were forever being passed back and forth from one regime to another. Before we'd gotten used to a new language and a new set of laws, it was time for the next. No one cared about our godforsaken territory, and so our roads were like the trousers of an adopted child—tattered, torn, and full of holes. Bumps and potholes and shaky bridges rattled the traveler to the core. But as there was no other way to get around, we put up with the suffocating dust in summer, the waist-high mud in autumn, the winter snows so deep that the route couldn't be seen at all. At the end of every trip, before resting our weary bones, we'd run to the synagogue to recite the blessing one says after escaping a great danger. It was on these roads that we traveled, and on these roads that the drivers earned their miserable living, never losing faith in the Eternal despite all their hardships—and never missing an opportunity to poke fun at the poor peasants they overtook along the way, trudging behind their teams of oxen.

The only markers on the roads were the wells near the Moldovan villages. They were adorned with crucifixes and blessed by the priest, and people went there with their holy pictures to pray for rain. The Jewish drivers stopped at these wells only to water their horses, of course. If they sneaked a drink themselves once in a while, surely they made no blessing over it. And if they did make a blessing sometimes . . . well, at this point who can know?

❖ ❖ ❖

A dirt road led from our town of Zguriţa to Drochia, the closest train station, which was far out of town, beyond the mill, beyond Shimenovitsh's place, near the village of

Nicorești, and on this dirt road stood one of God's mira-
cles. At the top of a steep hill was a level field, a clearing
where both men and beasts could catch their breath, and
in the very middle of this clearing, wonder of wonders,
stood an extraordinary nut tree. No one knew who had
planted it. Perhaps long ago a nut was carried here by the
wind, and the rains watered the ground at precisely the
right time, and a sprout took root and began to grow, and
nothing disturbed it, until at last the trunk rose high, high
into the air, spreading its healthy branches in a magnificent circle, like an umbrella. As big and beautiful as the
tree was, though, its fruits were small and shriveled. Wild
nuts, we called them, acorns. Impossible to eat. No doubt
God had made them inedible on purpose, so that instead
of climbing the tree and breaking its branches, people
would rest in its shade, enjoying its beauty and praising
the wisdom of the Almighty.

This was the tree we called the bridegroom tree. I don't
know about other towns, but in Zgurița every nickname—
whether for a person, a cow, even a tree in the field—was an
exact fit, as smooth and sharp-edged as a pane cut by a master glazier. Weddings were frequent in our town, all of them
pretty much the same. The same rabbi always officiated at
the same synagogue, the one with the red bricks. The same
Vaysbukh and his klezmer band always led the bride and
groom through the same streets. If the family was rich, each
guest got a quarter of a chicken; if not so rich, two people
had to share a quarter; and so on down the line, whatever
the host could manage. What made for a special occasion
was a groom from out of town—not an actual foreigner, of
course; everyone was from Bessarabia—but someone from
another *shtetl*. In such a case, the hustle and bustle began

early in the morning. The list of who would go to greet the groom was always drawn up weeks before, but every time it turned out at the last minute that a few important guests had been left out, and since such an insult would never be forgiven, another team and driver would be rustled up. No one breathed easy until all the close relations, mostly young people, were seated in the wagons festooned with bells, streamers, and flowers, shrieking with laughter, waiting for the signal to set out. The bridegroom tree was on everyone's lips. This was its day.

"Don't forget to serve the cakes and brandy at the bridegroom tree!"

"Don't forget to get out and swap seats with the groom's guests at the bridegroom tree!"

"At the bridegroom tree! At the bridegroom tree!"

The father of the bride kept waving his arms and yelling about the bridegroom tree, as if everyone didn't already know it was the official meeting-place. Here the members of the groom's party would get down from the wagons to stretch their legs and smooth their wrinkled clothing, unhitch one of the horses, and send a rider to announce their arrival. The row of coaches from the bride's side would then fly to the tree at a wild gallop. Oh, the brandy and cakes, the flowers, and the joy—all this the tree had witnessed in its flourishing years. No one suspected that before long the tree would share in the bitter fate of the Jews.

❧ ❧ ❧

After Ester returned from Siberia, it was a year before she could bring herself to visit her hometown. Finally, having explained to her husband a thousand times how to care for the baby, she took her coat and handbag and set off. People had told her over and over that there was no reason to hurry, nothing left to see. But the more she heard the word "nothing," the more she wanted to see that frightful "nothing" with her own eyes. And so she went.

After many hours, the bus came to a sudden stop near a makeshift sign. "Zgurița!" the driver called out in an unfamiliar accent, and Ester jumped up, startled. The driver was used to passengers like her, people returning after the war to grieve and cry. "Zgurița!" he said again, and the moment she stepped down he closed the door and took off, leaving her standing alone in the middle of a field. She took another look at the sign nailed to a pole. It looked like a scarecrow, with only the black hat missing. She gave a deep sigh and started off along the path toward the scattering of houses in the distance.

This, it appeared, was all that remained of her home-town. She'd felt the pain coming on as the bus sped along the highway. The name of a story had emerged all at once from the depths of her childhood memory, and all during the trip she couldn't get it out of her mind. "*Tiskhadesh!*" it was called—"Wear It in Good Health!" The story appeared in a schoolbook she'd read as a girl. Time and again, she'd wept over the tale of the poor little boy who never had new clothes, the boy who yearned to hear those syllables: "*Tiskhadesh*—wear it in good health." Finally he died, and his body was wrapped in a shroud, and then at last the angels did sing to him as he had wished. But by then it was too late, he couldn't hear them.

"*Tiskhadesh, Zgurița, tiskhadesh!*"

She walked faster, struggling to hold back tears. Don't cry, she told herself, don't cry. Just look, look and remember. She waded into a sea of weeds, and sure enough, there was Izak Koyfman's well, instantly recognizable by its pointy roof and the earthen perimeter that Izak was too stingy to plaster or whitewash. Izak always yelled and cursed at the locals who came to the well on hot summer days to cool off by splashing one another with pitchers of water. They cursed back, but he was too deaf to hear a word, which made them laugh and laugh. Now the well was barely visible in the tall grass. The roof was rusted, the earthen bench in ruins. Ester bent back the thorny stalks and stepped closer. She tried the crank, but it wouldn't turn. Counting her steps, she paced away from the well and soon found the place where her own house had stood. Only the cellar remained. If she hadn't been afraid to go down the stairs, no doubt she could have found the two iron iceboxes, one for dairy and the other for meat, but the yawning black maw of the cellar was too frightening, and she turned away. Back on the road, she stumbled onto a rusty grid and knew she must have reached Borekh Privman's yard, because only the hardware man could afford an iron lid on his slop pail. Here was the stone railing from Aunt Liba's front porch, where her mother and aunt would sit in the evenings when their work was done, never tiring of telling the same stories again and again. They were both long gone, and neither of them had been properly buried in a Jewish cemetery. So much for the railing.

Wandering from stone to stone through the graveyard of her girlhood, before she knew it she'd reached the bridge, which shook and creaked under her feet. Suddenly she remembered the bridegroom tree. How could she have forgotten? To tell the truth, she'd never once been

among those sent to greet the groom. In the first place she
was too young, so others were always picked before her.
Besides, she was considered a progressive thinker who
didn't believe in backward customs. Nonetheless, the tree
had a special meaning for her. It was here in the clearing
that she'd last laid eyes on her town. And it was here at
the bridegroom tree that her parents had said goodbye to
Zgurița for the last time.

The date was the fourteenth of June, 1941.

✦ ✦ ✦

She remembers.

It started with a knock, an ordinary knock on the outer
door at one o'clock in the morning. Her father hadn't
slept a wink since the arrests of so-called "undesirable
elements" had begun under the new Soviet power. Ears
pricked to detect the slightest rustle, he sprang instantly
from his bed and went into the foyer.

"Who is it?"

"Open up, Reb Hersh—it's me, Berl Royfe."

At the sound of a familiar voice, her father heaved a sigh
of relief and unlocked the door—and in they came, five
big NKVD police in jodhpurs and boots, hands on their
holsters in case of resistance. At the sight of a trembling
old man with a white beard, they let go of their revolvers.
"All right, Pop, don't panic," they said gruffly. "Quit crying
and turn on the light. Everybody put on your clothes and
get out in the street."

"Everybody?"

"Everybody."

"But why? What did we do? Where are we going?"

"No questions, Pop! *Davay, davay*, hurry up."

The short time they were given to prepare for the journey Ester remembers as one big nightmare. Of all the children, only she, the youngest daughter, was at home. She remembers the chaos, the tablecloths and bedsheets they spread out to bundle up their linens and clothing, the doors and drawers opened wide. Some of the men helped them empty the closets and pile everything on the floor. She remembers how her father wandered from room to room without picking up anything, and how he kept looking at Mother with a silent question in his eyes. One moment he was at the back door leading to the yard, and the next moment he was back in the room. Again to the door, then back. Only later did Ester learn that after his store was liquidated he'd hidden all the money under a brick in the chicken coop. Too frightened to go out to the yard and retrieve it, he lost everything he'd earned in all his years of hard work. She remembers Berl Royfe, pale as death, signing the official report attesting that everything had been done according to the rules, after which they carried their bundles into the street.

Outside it was pitch black. The streetlights had been turned off. All was still as a grave. Not a creature was about. Only the wagon waited in front of the house. The chief secured their door with a padlock, put the key in his pocket, and signaled to the peasant driver to get a move on. When they reached the bridge, silhouettes of other wagons began to emerge from the darkness, all headed in the same direction. Apparently they were not the only ones.

Day began to break.

"Uncle Hersh!" a voice called out.

"Rivkele, you too? Where are the children?"

"Right here, sleeping. Grandma is with us, too."

Seated in the wagon was eighty-year-old Aunt Gitl, wrapped in a thick shawl despite the summer heat. Here were Borekh Gurvitz and Lipa Lifshitz and their wives, and Velvl Gelman, Shmuel Gotloyber, Avromke Shilkroyt, Kuni Stolyer, and Khaim Litvak—Jews and more Jews, all on the list of "bourgeois elements" that the local authorities had quickly pulled together on orders from above. These were the ones being rounded up for *spetspereselenye*—"special resettlement."

Unaware of the great calamity that was to come, the victims could think only of their own misfortune. Why, they asked, why us?

One after another the wagons crossed the bridge, leaving behind the mill and Shimenovitsh's place. The horses panted as they pulled the heavy wagons up the hill. Never before had people ridden up the hill; to spare the horses, they'd always gotten off and walked. Now they were strictly forbidden to get down. When they reached the clearing, the wagons pulled up all in a row to make it easier to keep watch, and only then were they allowed off. Everyone crowded together.

"What's happening? Where are they taking us? What will happen to the children?"

"Who knows?"

"Why are we just standing here?"

"What's the rush? We've already missed the train."

Now wagons were arriving from the surrounding villages, all of them loaded with wooden crates full of the peasants' belongings, along with sacks of potatoes, cornmeal, and wheat from last year's harvest.

"Why didn't we think of that? We were afraid to bring too much."

"Never mind, they're in for it just like us."

"Nah, they'll have an easier time of it, they're used to hard labor. But us—"

"God will provide."

"He has already provided."

Suddenly a murmur swept through the crowd. Had some official arrived? But no, it was Rasya Rabinovitsh, clever, educated Rasya, whose husband the Zionist had been the first one arrested. Rasya, the pride and joy of her family and of the whole town, was running around waving her arms and crying: "We're at the bridegroom tree, everyone! The groom is almost here! Bring out the cakes and brandy! Why isn't anyone doing anything?" She tore the shawl off her head, releasing her thick black curls. Tears streamed down her cheeks as she began to sing the traditional wedding song: "All together, all together, let us greet the groom . . ."

Her mother, Tova, went to her side. "What are you saying, child? For God's sake, calm down."

"It's no use, Mama. It's all over!"

"God in Heaven, why are You silent?"

✦ ✦ ✦

Ester breathed heavily as she climbed the hill to the clearing. Where was the tree? She could see it in the distance—what was left of it, that is. Half of it was lying on the ground. The other half was still standing, withered and crooked like a question mark, its surviving branches twisted to the left, as if they were trying to protect the rest, bent over the way a dog curls up to lick a wound on its hindquarters.

She knew about the great tragedy that had happened here when the war broke out, soon after she and her parents had been taken away. The Jews had scattered in all directions, trying to escape. Some tried to cross the Dniester at Soroca, others ran to catch a train in Drochia. Suddenly, here in the clearing, the buzz of approaching airplanes was heard, and everyone rushed to the tree for shelter. A bomb from a thundering Messerschmidt split the tree in two, burying those who'd taken cover underneath.

So it would be for anyone who attempted to give shelter to the Jews.

RESTING PLACE

Great and mighty is the Ob River. Swollen with many years of experience, it flows sedately, without haste, as if it knows what awaits at the end of the journey to the Far North and so chooses to linger, enjoying the fleeting pleasures of summer while they last, and though it never actually manages to warm up, at least it has a chance to play with the sparkling sunbeams before they flit off into the dense Siberian forest. Utterly dependent on the river, the Siberians show their respect by making the short name longer: *Batyushka Ob*, they say—Father Ob, our provider and protector! But Father pays no mind to their pleas and their flattery. He does as he wishes, when he wishes. Like a father, he provides nourishment, and like a father, he punishes with all his strength. Over the years, the locals have learned all his tricks. They know how to handle him even in the stormiest times when he rises up in a rage,

lips foaming savagely as he breaks out of the icy armor
that has shackled him all winter and lifts ice floes as big
as houses high into the air. In this season he is terrible
in his madness. He overflows his banks, inundates and
annihilates, uproots and destroys, and carries away everything in his path—trees, houses, rafts, lost cows. Then he
sucks into his vortex the bravest and the most daring of
the Siberians—not only the young and not only men—
challenging them to pit their agility against his diabolical
strength, to see who will win and who will reap the spoils.
Not for the victory but for the booty, they risk their lives
by pushing off one by one in their pointy canoes—*shlupky*,
they call them, or *chelnoky*—armed with ropes, chains,
and long hooked poles for grabbing the precious building
materials that are hard to come by any other way: beams,
planks, rafters, logs, blocks, lumber of every shape and
size. In pursuit of their prey, they stand up in their little
boats, swaying and tottering in their battle with the terrible floes. Catch sight of them, even from a distance, and
your head will spin.

◆ ◆ ◆

To this region, a great barge transports the latest batch of
deportees, who are known as *spetspereselentsy*, or "special
settlers"—a long, complicated name for women and children. The men, the heads of households, have long since
been separated from them, and God only knows where
they are and what's happened to them. All of them on the
barge are feeling seasick even though it's the beginning of
August, when the Ob flows quietly and calmly within its
high banks. The river is so wide that those banks cannot

be seen from the barge. They're off beyond the horizon, the subject of fervent prayers. God in Heaven, have You condemned us to wander without end? Will we never reach the shore?

After weeks in the stinking boxcars, with their narrow barred windows up near the ceiling and a chamber pot in the middle of the floor, without a breath of air or a mouthful of food—after that, a remote Siberian collective farm called "New Way," a settlement consisting of a few dozen houses, had been their first resting place. Here they'd been allowed to stretch their legs, take a look around, wash off, and fill their lungs with gulps of fresh air. They were even happy to work in the fields, trying to hoe potatoes without hitting either the potatoes themselves or, worse, their own feet. But before long the officials with the tight trousers showed up and ordered them to resume their journey. No doubt the genius in charge of things had decided it was too risky to bring brand-new special settlers into contact with worn-out collective farmers.

For more than a week now, the barge has been moving slowly upon the Ob, on and on with no end in sight. People say the boat must not be moving at all, just standing still, because all they can see is water and sky, sky and water. The barge is a matchbox in the void, its passengers crammed head to head like matches, along with their children, their elderly, their baggage. Some stay up on deck, others down in the hold. A debate rages over who is worse off, but what's the difference? They're all miserable. As in the boxcars, they're covered with lice, fighting over every inch of space, quarreling over nothing, their spirits low. They have no idea when, how, or even if they will ever get out of this place.

Then Shprintse comes up with a clever idea. Every morning, as people are struggling to emerge from their nighttime despair, she begins describing her dreams in minute detail. Bit by bit, everyone quiets down, and a crowd gathers. Carefully she adds a slight shade here, a bit of color there. People believe every word. Why would she lie? The familiar names and places she evokes with such precision, and the good omens she never fails to see, are a balm for sore hearts. Even when it all sounds a little suspicious, everyone goes along with the game. No one challenges her. Shprintse has always been renowned for her eloquence, her rich, juicy language full of quotations and proverbs, her ability to describe situations so vividly you can see them before your very eyes. No one interrupts, no one protests that she's exaggerating. Everyone is all ears, listening with pleasure and begging for more. All the stories end the same way: "Have faith, children, the God who led our forefathers out of Egypt will rescue us from this place, *bimheyre beyemeynu*, speedily in our days, amen!"

In this way she gets the day off to a good start—though not for long. Soon enough, the privation and crowding take over. Yet even when tempers fray, the Jews of Zgurița stick together, a little apart from the others. Interestingly, the peasants from the neighboring villages also stay close by, not quite mingling with the Jews but not letting them out of sight either. They recognize the faces from the Thursday market, the language is familiar, and beyond that, they believe that in times of need it's always a good idea to stick with a Jew, because one way or another a Jew will come up with a way to get by. So they stay close, and if asked politely, they'll even "lend" a handful of cornmeal

for a pot of comforting *mamaliga*. Foolish peasants! They
don't realize that at this point everyone is in the same pre-
dicament, that the weight of the unknown presses equally
on one and all, and that all anyone wants is to get out of
this hell, off this barge, as quickly as possible, it doesn't
matter where, any place where they can feel the earth
under their feet.

On top of everything else—the pimple on the boil,
as they say—there's the old lady. Having lived for nearly
ninety years in Zgurița, Madam Garber has chosen the
barge as her deathbed. Back at the collective farm, it
was obvious that her time was near, and now it's clear
she won't survive for more than a day or two. So be it,
a person doesn't live forever. But what if she closes her
eyes before the barge gets to shore? The officials might
well order her thrown overboard. Anxiously the Jews beg
God to have mercy, to delay her last breath and allow her
a proper burial. On account of Madam Garber, in fact,
their group is first off the barge when they finally drop
anchor in the godforsaken place with a sign atop a pole:
Kipryushka.

✦ ✦ ✦

If the chemical works in the forest where they're headed
is a living hell, Kipryushka is the antechamber. The settlement is long and thin, ten or twelve houses along a
brook with the same name. It's like the neck of a bottle;
once you're inside, it's hard to get out. Maybe Kipryushka
doesn't deserve such a bad name—after all, the settlement itself is not to blame for the fate of the deportees—but in the eyes of these dejected people, everyone

and everything is at fault. The settlers are *starovyery*, Old Believers—robust Russians with red beards and even redder fat cheeks, who won't allow the new arrivals to enter their houses or drink water from their precious cups. Anyone who complains, hoping to arouse a little sympathy, receives the same answer: "*Privyknete*, you'll get used to it." They tell how they themselves were brought here ten years ago, in the first deportation, which they refer to as the *raskulachivanye*, when the kulaks, the more prosperous peasants who resisted being sent to the collective farms, were sent into exile. They were dumped in the forest, which was then totally uninhabited, and left to survive however they could. Many died, but the healthiest young people got to work chopping down trees and building houses, and today they live quite well, with a cow, a pig, chickens. Thank God, they say, crossing themselves, they have nothing to complain about. They won't let anyone take them away from here, they say with a laugh. To hear them tell it, they've been blessed with good fortune.

Meanwhile, the deportees sit on their bundles under the open sky, swatting at mosquitoes and wishing for something to eat. The dry bread is hard to swallow even when they wash it down with hot water. Now the Moldovans turn out to be not so foolish after all. With no help from the Jews, they come up with the idea of planting themselves on the settlers' doorsteps and crossing themselves until they're given food. What can the Jews do? They can't kiss the *mezuzahs* on the doorposts—there are no *mezuzahs*. Instead they trade a new shirt or a pair of trousers for a bowl of potatoes, some onions, a little milk, and they make a fire and cook dinner. After they eat, as if they were observing *tashlikh,* the Rosh Hashanah ritual in which Jews empty their pockets into a flowing stream, they go down the hill to the brook, take off their clothes, and drown the lice in the water.

Madam Garber has been installed in a room belonging to one of the Russians. It took tearful entreaties and a sum of money, but at least now she has a roof over her head. She lies on a bed of straw waiting for death. Her two daughters, themselves getting on in years, sit on either side in silence. For one thing, there's nothing to say, and for another, they've been quarreling for years and are not on speaking terms. It has something to do with an amber necklace—or maybe it was pearl—and possibly something else that one of them, but not the other, received for her wedding. It's all ancient history by now; they're both well-off—rich enough to be deported! But the injustice can't be forgiven; they're still angry and want nothing to do with each other. Sheyndl, the older one, is miserable because she didn't bring any valuables with her from home, the way others did, and now she has nothing to trade. Her children are old enough to have helped, but they didn't, and now they carp at her as if it's all her fault, pointing out that her sister, their aunt, is walking around with her bosom bulging, no doubt hiding all of Grandma's jewelry in her blouse. So the two sisters sit by the bed, sulking, and no one tries to intervene; it would be pointless. Even when their mother finally breathes her last, the two remain silent. But now others take over, lowering the body to the floor, boiling water, washing the corpse and wrapping it in a white sheet, placing candles at the head.

Escorting a person to his eternal rest is always a sad occasion, but at the same time, there's something about the cemetery full of relatives, the traditional ceremony

overseen by the burial society, the eulogies full of praise,
the loud wailing—all of this is bound to make at least some
of the mourners feel envious of the dead person, especially if it's a rich dead person with a magnificent funeral.
Now imagine the sorry huddle of women and children
who are performing the rites for the dead for the first time
in their lives. They have no choice—there is no one else to
do it. They lower the body into the ground and cover the
grave. Then they look at one another, wondering what to
do next. They hang their heads in embarrassment. The
silence goes on for so long that it begins to grate on the
ears, suggesting a disrespect for the dead and for whatever
sense of self-worth remains inside them.

Ester feels it in the very core of her being. She looks at
the women around her who are staring into the freshly
dug grave as if they're trying to figure out who is worse
off, Madam Garber or themselves. She sees the peasants
watching from a distance. Her heart aches for the fathers
so far away, for the helpless mothers, for the young people who will spend the best years of their lives in misery in the forest, for those who will end their days in the
taiga, for everyone around her, and all at once she forgets who she is, forgets that only men are permitted to
say the prayer for the dead. She lifts her head and begins
to recite the blessing the way her father would have: "*El
moley rakhmim*, God full of mercy, who dwells in the
heavens . . ." Everyone is shocked. "Give rest on the wings
of the Divine Presence, among the holy, pure and glorious
who shine like the sky, to the soul of . . . Madam Garber . . .
in Heaven . . ." Suddenly she stops. She lifts one shoulder.

Shprintse, her mother, knows why she broke off:
because the word "Madam" doesn't belong in a Jewish

blessing. "It doesn't matter, my child," she says, loud enough for everyone to hear. "It doesn't matter. If the Lord can allow us to be exiled to Siberia, then He'll have to learn some new languages, not just the holy tongue."

Hearing the words "exile" and "Siberia," the crowd erupts into a terrible wailing.

The ice has broken. Ester breathes more freely. She can't remember the rest of the prayer for the dead. She doesn't know any more of the words. But it doesn't matter. It doesn't matter.

BREAD

Every day at the break of dawn they arrive, the man and his horse—or should I say the horse and his man? The horse is so big, with sturdy hips rippling under a shining chestnut hide, that it could well be the boss of the little Yemeni man with his wispy beard and long side curls.

The horse apparently needs no whip; it goes straight to the rubbish bins and stops as if to say, "Here we are, now do your job." The man doesn't have to be told twice. He jumps down from the cart and gets to work. First he picks out a good-sized roll and offers it to his esteemed partner. The horse accepts the roll with dignity, sniffing all sides of it while reciting the *hamotzi* blessing in the language of horses, then chomps away with its big teeth while the man goes about expertly collecting and sorting, filling the row of cardboard boxes in the wagon: one with bread, one with challah, others with rolls, buns, pitas, even day-old home-baked pastries—all the leftovers that the spoiled, empty-headed Children of Israel think they're too good for.

What does he do with the bread? It doesn't matter, so long as he takes it away—away from the rubbish, away from the stray cats scrounging in the bins, away from all who might look with pity and sorrow on the tragedy of bread taking place daily in this country.

When the man's work is done, he waits patiently for the horse to shake its head—a sign that it has finished the blessing for the close of its meal—before they move on to the next bin.

As I watch them leave, pictures appear before me, pictures engraved in my memory, pictures that will accompany me to the end of my days.

❖ ❖ ❖

1943. The height of World War II. A howl of lamentation resounds from one end of Russia to the other. Death knocks ceaselessly at our doors, delivering brown envelopes with official stamps bringing news that a father or son has "fallen heroically on the battlefield in fulfillment of his duty to the Fatherland." The bereaved wail to the heavens, split the skies with their cries, writhe in pain—and early the next morning they take their place in the *ochered*, the breadline.

Bread—bread is holy! Bread waits for no man. *Bread* rhymes with *dead*. In those years, the last thing likely to appear before a person's eyes as he takes his final breath is a slice of bread.

As soon as you get to the head of the line, you become nothing more than a pair of eyes. No power on earth can make you stop watching the woman's hands as she checks your cards and weighs out your family's share for the day—500 grams for workers, 200 for everyone else. The bread is sticky and heavy, a mixture of bran and potatoes, but you're used to it, as if you've never eaten any other kind. All you care about is getting your portion. Every extra crumb kindles a spark of hope in your heart—a hope against hope.

Meanwhile, everyone is gathered around the table waiting for Mother, and when she arrives, it's the same thing again: all eyes, big and small, are fixed on her hands as she divides the loaf. The crumbs that break off during the slicing of your portion belong to you, and you're not embarrassed about scraping them up and putting them straight into your mouth so as not to lose them. You don't worry that others will laugh or call you greedy, because everyone does the same thing. You hold the crumbs in your mouth for a long time, chewing and sucking, without taking your eyes off Mother's hands as they continue slicing and dividing. No one moves until all the bread has been distributed. Only then do you swallow—not noticing, or at least pretending not to notice, that the very last portion, the one Mother has left for herself, is smaller than anyone else's. No one mentions it—that's the way it is with mothers. Since the adults are in a hurry to get to work, the soup is brought straight to the table. Spirits rise, especially when a chunk of beet or potato shows up along with the millet. Fragrant steam rises from the earthen bowls, and wooden spoons dance before your eyes. You slurp up the soup, the hotter the better, scalding your tongue and smacking your lips.

You don't eat the bread yet. You eat the soup first while the bread is toasting on the stove. Every piece is laid out just so, and you can turn any charred crust into roasted meat or pastry or whatever you wish—all you have to do is close your eyes and remember the old days back home.

You know you ought to divide your piece in two and save half for the evening meal, but it's hard to resist temptation when you're hungry. You pinch off a little piece, then a little more, and even more, until it's gone. You sigh, but at the same time you pat your belly as if to say, "I'm full now—let God worry about tomorrow." After an hour or two, though, the meager meal has disappeared as if it was never there, and you're hungry again. You try to subdue the pangs with work or play, but the chunk of bread you should have saved sticks in your mind. If only you had it now, even a tiny piece! You berate yourself in the worst terms and solemnly swear that tomorrow ... Yet when tomorrow comes you're hungrier than ever, and once again you can't hold out. You resign yourself to your fate and your "weak character." Even a child knows that each of us receives our portion according to what is *polozheno*— officially allotted—which is like what we say in Hebrew, *min hashamayim*, ordained in Heaven. So you accept the verdict without complaining or crying or asking for more.

❖ ❖ ❖

In those bitter days, we'd been scattered to the ends of the earth, exiled to Siberia for our own or our parents' supposed transgressions. We were the lost tribe, the deportees. Once upon a time, we'd been lovely brides and schoolgirls, shielded from the slightest breath of wind. After two years of hard labor, it was hard to recognize us as those same young ladies. We spent all day in the forest dressed in rags, our trousers held up with twine, faces covered with masks against mosquitoes, buckets and shovels in our hands. Starving, exhausted, isolated from all human contact, we had the feeling that the Lord Himself had gotten lost somewhere up in the tall, dense crowns of the pine trees and completely abandoned us. It was left to God's deputy, our *nachalnik*, to rule over us according to the law of the taiga, by force. He was fully prepared to rip our hearts out for the slightest infraction. Our hearts—as if he of all people had anything to do with our hearts. But if he took away our portion of bread . . . oh, then he could make us truly wretched—and have more for himself. So we had to throw the dog a bone, flatter him by addressing him by his full title, and rush to obey whatever order happened to cross his mind: to chop and carry his wood, light the fire in his stove, do his laundry, clean his room, scour his floor with sand until it shone. We did everything we could to soften him up, hoping that when he weighed the buckets of resin we'd worked so hard to collect he wouldn't be too strict, and that when he measured the wood we'd sawed and chopped he'd overlook the pieces of bark we sneaked in here and there.

Besides bread, twice a day, morning and evening, the kitchen gave us soup made from the dregs of soaking barley-straw. The soup was hot and it stuck to our ribs, quieting our hunger for at least a short time. On top of that, we ate whatever we could find in the forest. Into the sacks hanging from our shoulders went mushrooms, *kolba* (wild garlic that was said to guard against scurvy), and above all, berries: currants, blackberries, lingonberries, wood sorrel, and others whose names I've forgotten, thank God. The berries were our manna, but with a difference. Rather than falling from the heavens, this manna had to be collected from swamps and marshes, and in order to find it you had to walk with your head down, eyes fixed on the ground. Alas, people often wandered deep into the forest, lost their way, and never returned. This is what happened to my mother, of blessed memory. On the twentieth of August, 1943, she went into the forest to gather berries, and she will remain in the taiga to the end of time. When I came home from work and realized what had happened, I screamed at the top of my lungs. Everyone from our district, led by our boss, headed into the woods to look for my mother. We carried lanterns, sticks, and a rifle. We yelled and banged and whistled and shot off the gun, listening for a response—all in vain. Late at night we returned empty-handed. Exhausted from weeping and shouting, I went into our little room. When I lay down on the bed we shared, I felt something under my head. I lifted the pillow and burst into tears. There, wrapped in a white handkerchief, was the crust of bread my mother had been saving for later.

Forty-three years have passed since then, and only now do I confess that I ate my mother's bread that night. I soaked the crust with bitter tears and I devoured it.

❖ ❖ ❖

Now I look out into the early morning and I wonder: my God, how many lives could be saved with the bread we throw away every day? I think of the moist white loaves of braided challah we have on Shabbos. We put them on the table in a place of honor, we cover them with a white embroidered cloth, we light the candles and we say a blessing over them ... and the next day we toss those very challahs in the garbage. Why, I ask, why do we even bother to bless them?

ALONE

Siberian frost
Oh, how you chill us
Spare me and my horse,
Please, do not kill us!
—Russian folksong

Galya turns her shoulders from side to side, positioning the straps in the middle of her back, then tugs them tight and fastens them expertly across her chest. During these years in Siberia she has mastered the art of harnessing herself to a sled so that she pulls the load not with her arms but with her whole body, like a horse. To boost her spirits and curb her fear, she imitates a horse by playfully kicking up her feet in her big felt boots. She even attempts a whinny, but old Vasily cuts her off sternly. "*Ne baloy, devka,*" he says—"Quit it, girl. You have a long, hard road ahead of you." He opens the gate. "*S'bogom!*—Go with God!"

"Goodbye, Uncle Vasily!" Galya bids him farewell in the local fashion: "Speak me no ill!" She waves her big glove and sets off.

Outside, day is just breaking, but the sparkling white path stretches out clearly before her. From time to time she can hear a door creaking or see a gleam of fire through a frost-covered window, but most of the village is still deep in sleep. The houses look like gnomes in a children's story, with pointy white caps pulled down over their ears as they puff on their pipes. Instead of lingering over the rooftops, the smoke from the chimneys rises straight up into the sky—a sign of the bitter cold. No wonder that when Vasily came inside at dawn hitching up his trousers, he muttered, "*Krepchayet,*" it's getting worse, which prompted his wife, Auntie Pasha, to scold him for upsetting Galya just as she was setting out.

"Fool!" she said. "Get back up on the oven if your ass is so cold."

"Yours looks nice and fat," he said.

"Shut your trap," she said, "or I swear—"

"No swearing on an empty stomach, old woman, you'll curdle the food."

"Never mind, you'll eat it up and ask for more."

A stranger might have thought the two were about to tear each other to pieces, but Galya could tell they were just expressing their affection, Siberian style. No Siberian, especially an old man, ever praised his wife, even when he knew she deserved a medal for rising at dawn when everyone else was still in bed, getting the fire started and filling the big cast-iron pots with icy water, chilblains and all.

As she walks, Galya remembers the scene and smiles. Despite their angry words, she envies the couple, not so much for herself but on behalf of her parents, who were separated at the very time when they most needed each other. First they were evicted from their home and deported without a why or wherefore. Then the men were taken away from their families to prevent any possibility of revolt. Interesting to think about the geniuses who spend their days dreaming up new ways to torture people. But this is not the time or place for such thoughts. There's nothing worse than tears in the bitter cold. Better to register complaints against the Lord in a safer place—sitting at home, for example, or even better, lying in bed under warm covers, perhaps on Sunday morning, when you don't have to go to work and can indulge in the luxury of speculating about the ways of the world.

> God, Your judgment must we praise
> Never questioning Your ways
> Dreadful though the pain we bear
> Your design is always fair
> God, Your judgment must we praise!

These days, Galya's mother is silent. She no longer sings the snatches of old theater songs as she used to, no matter how busy she was with the housework. Now she says little. What does her clever mother think about God and His judgment now—if indeed she thinks about Him at all? But walking in the forest, Galya wants nothing to do with the Lord of the Universe. Let Him stay up there in the sky, His right hand guiding her and keeping her safe—her and the food she managed to scrounge over the past few days as she went from door to door in the village. Beyond that, let Him keep His distance. But enough complaining, enough self-pity. She's not the only one suffering.

What time is it by now? About six, she estimates, or six-thirty, maybe seven. Hard to say. The frozen moon has just poked her nose out, impatient for Her Highness the Sun to relieve her so she can hurry off somewhere to warm up. Foolish moon. In her place, Galya would hibernate all winter like a bear, and no one would miss her dim light, her meager warmth. No one in Siberia cares about reciting the blessing in honor of the moon—and besides, you're not allowed to anymore. Now a sentry stands guard at night, and the moon, frozen in place in the heavens, is of no use at all, not even to couples in love. Who can kiss with frozen lips? Galya smiles, imagining a pair of sweethearts with white frozen noses trying to kiss by the light of the moon. Kissing—at twenty, she's long since forgotten the taste of a kiss on the lips. How can she think about love when she's struggling to survive? It's a good thing none of her former admirers can see her in her present get-up. With that, she straightens up and adjusts the scarf covering her forehead so that it won't slip as she strains to pull the sled. Ridiculous! Who could she possibly run into here? Yet she wouldn't turn down a traveling companion, nor feel embarrassed in his presence—he wouldn't look any better himself. A companion would be welcome, actually. Not because she's afraid of walking alone. What is there to be afraid of? Bandits are unheard of in these parts. They're after rich victims, and here no one has more than a sack of potatoes to his name. Wild animals? They stay away from the roads, and even if she did meet up with one, it wouldn't help much to have someone else by her side. But she doesn't want to think about wild animals. There aren't any, that's all. No birds, either. Not a one. So why does the forest warden from Section Three go out hunting with his dog, Laika, every day? There's nothing he likes more. He knows the forest like the back of his hand and ventures far from the beaten path in pursuit of rabbits, squirrels, gophers, and maybe larger animals, too—but she doesn't want to think about those. No, there are no wild animals on the roads. So why would she want someone by her side? Just for the companionship? Maybe he'd make her lose her train of thought, or complain about having nothing to trade, or try to impress her with tales of his business deals, or ask her questions. She doesn't like being grilled. The only person she wants to confide in is her mother, who always responds with a warm smile and a hug: "Good for you, Goldele, darling!"

Oh, Mama, if you knew how cold I am!

The weather has worsened. The sun is shining, but its teeth bite and burn without mercy. Galya pulls her hands out of her gloves and rubs her frozen cheeks, as Auntie Pasha has warned her a thousand times never to do. Auntie has also told her never to cover her mouth with her scarf, no matter how cold it gets. If the steam from her mouth freezes to the scarf, she's finished, Auntie says. "A *goy* prolongs the Exile"—so say the Jews even in the best of times. Come to think of it, whose idea was the Exile in the first place? But again, better not to think about such things. She doesn't want to quarrel with God today. Even bosses less important than He don't like it when you ask too many questions.

What will she tell Mother when she gets home? First, that she's held on to what she started out with, she's traded well and come out more or less even. Since most people don't have enough to eat, they want no part of "beggars" like Galya and try to drive her off like a dog before she can open her mouth. Even those who do have something don't know what to ask for in return. Scarves, trousers, vests—but where is she to find such things? Nonetheless she's gotten the hang of it—she's a shopkeeper's daughter, after all. To the tired old merchandise no one wants, she adds a spool of thread, a bit of ribbon or floss left over from the old haberdashery store. There's no sense bargaining over needles—anyone who owns one keeps it safely stuck into the embroidered cloth in the icon corner and hardly ever uses it. The women on the collective farms aren't much good at repairing a garment, sewing a patch, or darning a sock. They stitch up a hole any which way, wielding the needle as awkwardly as they hold a pen when they have to sign their names.

Meanwhile, the peasants carry on as if all is well. They have no complaints and put the entire blame for their poverty on the war. It's hard to say how things were before the war, but now the wind whistles over the empty shelves at the store, and all that remains of yesterday's "riches" are jars of Metamorfoza skin cream, which the manager arranges and rearranges in various appealing pyramids. Even the Troynoy eau de cologne is gone, probably gulped down like whiskey. Nonetheless, a store is a store, even if there's a padlock on the door most of the time. Barbara Panteleimonovna, the manager, goes around with her nose in the air, talking loudly and jingling her keys, and everyone tries to get on her good side because she's on excellent terms with the regional officials. From time to time, a little something finds its way into her hands, and she's the one who decides who gets it.

What Mother will be most delighted by are the letters Galya wrote for the peasants to send to their sons at the front. It was thanks to these letters that the old couple invited her to sleep over and gave her a bowl of borsht with some delicious hot potatoes. Old Vasily doffed his cap, scratched his head, and made the sign of the cross as she read her words aloud. "*Ot dayot*," he said, "*ot sterva!*—I'll be damned! The little witch can write!"—which for him was the highest praise. She poured everything she had into the letters, every ounce of knowledge and imagination she could summon. First she extended greetings and regards from the whole extended family, neighbors, and friends, including the children and even the infants, patiently inscribing all their names. Then she got down to business describing the harvest they'd brought in, the cow that blessed them with as much milk as they needed, and how difficult it was for Father, given his age and his declining powers, to mow the grass—but enough, one must not complain, with God's help they would get through the hard times, the war would end and their sons would come home safe and sound.

It would be a shame to leave it at that, Galya felt, a missed opportunity. And so she plumbed her memory and threw in everything she could think of, even her mother's personal version of "God of Abraham," the blessing that closes the Sabbath. She asked the Lord Jesus to heal our wounded soldiers and to keep the healthy ones out of harm's way. She asked the Lord to release us from the war this year and to return our soldiers to us in victory. Amen! Then she thought for a while and decided that since she'd already sinned, she might as well keep going. The Gates of Heaven are open, she wrote, and may they never be locked; let our prayers and our pleas rise up and be received before the Throne of God.

At this point, old Vasily crossed himself and added more kerosene to the lamp so that she could read out the letter again. People craned their necks and watched with awe as the words streamed from her pen as if by magic. The lamp had been lit only for the sake of the letter, and after she had read it out for the second time, the light was extinguished, but people stayed on, talking over the letter by the gleam of the fire, without, Galya hoped, having the faintest notion of where the high-flown words had come from. The next evening, new clients showed up, wanting their own "heartfelt" letters, and carrying under their shawls a bit of kerosene for the lamp, a chunk of frozen milk for "the writer girl." Auntie Pasha, it seemed, insisted on these payments. Galya didn't concern herself with such matters. She was busy with her muse, producing one winged phrase after another.

What will Mother say about the letters? Oh, she'll be angry that her "God of Abraham" has been bestowed on the *goyim*, but Galya will tell her not to be silly. "There's no harm done, Mother," she'll say. "Obviously, what is for God is for God and what is for people is for people, but sometimes what's good for God is even better for people, and besides," she'll say, "people know how to appreciate a good word and pay for it on the spot, in cash, whereas in return for your virtuous prayers, God has rewarded you with nothing but a home in Siberia." Maybe she won't use those exact words, but this is what she will say. If only she could be arguing with Mother at this very moment!

Meanwhile her very heart and soul are freezing. She'll never get home to Mother today. She'll be lucky even to reach Section Three. By then she will have walked twenty-five kilometers in the bitter weather. Back home no one would have believed her capable of such a thing. From Section Three back home to Section Eight is at least another eleven or twelve kilometers. She'll never make it. No, she'll spend the night at Section Three with Masya, and Masya will give her a cup of hot tea with a little milk, not so much for the taste as to show that at their house they don't, God forbid, drink their hot water plain, the way others do, but always with a little milk. Look how clever she's become here in the forest! At home people considered her a bit of a simpleton, but it didn't matter, because as they say, if you're lucky you don't need to be clever. Section Three is coming up! It's right by the highway, not far at all. Maybe the postal sled will come through and she'll be able to hop on and hear the news and even make a trade. Oh, for a ride! Anything would be better than walking. The potatoes in the sled are covered with straw, but they're as cold as she is. It would be just her luck if they froze. But why be angry at everything and everybody, at those who deserve it and those who don't? It's because the gears in her head have started to freeze; they turn in only one direction. Enough! Better to look up, to gaze at the beauty of the forest in its splendid white raiment. An enchanted palace! Not a twig stirring. All is majestic, beautiful, white, silent, calm. The silence is maddening, though. She wants to scream and curse, to shatter this magic that has penetrated her bones down to the marrow. Mama, oh Mama! Her Highness the Sun shows herself for a moment, as snooty as Barbara Panteleimonovna jingling her keys, then disappears—*ot sterva*, the little witch!

But wait! She sees something in the road up ahead. It looks like—a sled! Thank God! A little late, perhaps, but it's already beginning to get dark, and she's so cold and tired that it will be good to feel a human breath nearby. But what . . . ? The sled isn't moving. She takes a step forward. Her heart begins to pound. The sled is stopped in the road and a person is lying on top, embracing the sack with both arms. Galya shudders. Asleep—in this weather? She goes closer and gives a nudge. Don't sleep, don't sleep. The person rolls off like a sack of potatoes and lies in the middle of the road, arms stretched out, palms facing the sky. Galya totters and grabs at the sled to keep from falling. Run! As soon as she straightens up, she understands, and all she can think to do is run. Run away if you want to stay alive! Save yourself! At the same time, a feverish impulse propels her toward the corpse. It's a person, after all, not a dead dog, and instead of continuing on her way she ought at least to take a look, even if there's nothing she can do. She takes another step and peers into the face. Sluva! At once she knows it's Sluva Shvartsman, her friend's mother from Section Six. There's no question. God! A wild shriek tears from her chest, shaking the forest for miles around. The trees awaken and roar back: God! Again she screams: What have You done? The echo comes: Done? Why do You persecute us? she demands. Whose side are You on, and who is Your enemy? Some by fire and some by water, it says in the Bible—is that no longer enough for You? Now You demand some by ice, too? I won't have it, do You hear? I won't have it! With her last strength she begins to run. She runs like one possessed. The sled bangs against her legs. She stumbles and falls, gets up and runs on. She's afraid to look back, afraid of being turned into a pillar of ice. The name rings in her ears: Sluva, Sluva! Then, suddenly, Slava, Slava! Why that? Ah, she understands: *slava*—Russian for *glory*, as in "Glory be to God!" When we hear of a death, we Jews say "Blessed is the True Judge." No, not true, He is not true. Sluva dead? Like this? Why? Galya falls again. Her scarf is stuck to her lips, stiff as a board. Afflict me, forget me, I am gone, I am already dead. Alone, alone will I run. Alone. On both sides of the road, the trees begin to move, to run toward her so as to strangle her in their branches. No, not in their branches—in their wings, their giant white wings. Wings of angels—and the angels, too, are crying: alone, alone, alone! Al-al-al! Woof-woof-woof! Laika's tongue licks her face, and there, behind the dog, on his great skis, stands the forest warden from Section Three.

THE PAYBACK

During the six or seven coldest months of the year, when the sap didn't run and resin production was suspended, Riva was my partner for a variety of forest jobs. To be honest, she was in charge and I was her assistant—her apprentice, really. I needed her to show me how to use the tools, how to approach a tree, chop it down, clean it, saw it, split the logs, and stack them so well that the boss could find nothing to criticize. Even as an apprentice I was no good. I mean it—no matter how I tried, the saw kept getting stuck in the wood, and I could never pull it out by myself. Poor Riva would have to make a wedge and pound it in to free the blade. I don't know what went through her head while she was doing this, but what she said out loud was that I was trying too hard. "Don't lean on the saw," she'd say. "Take it easy." She could tell I didn't really understand.

How could I ever have believed that chopping wood and carrying water were simple jobs that required no brains at all?

Besides chopping, she was better at stacking, too, so I bowed to her superior ability and handed her the split logs one by one. She would construct the cubic meter like an engineer, slipping in some bark so cleverly that the boss would never notice. Here I made my contribution. Holding up a twig, I pretended to be a priest and solemnly blessed the stack while intoning the Jesus Prayer in a deep voice. Riva would choke back giggles. She never laughed out loud.

We didn't always feel so playful. More often not. Sometimes the tree we were working on was so gnarled and knotty that it simply wouldn't yield to the ax, and the bitter cold licked at us with its icy tongue. At those times we didn't joke. Eyes glazed, I would look around me and curse the day I was born. If the two of us hadn't been working together, I could never have held out. I would have given up and forfeited my bread ration. Not Riva. Without a word or a glance in my direction, she bit her lip and kept at it, and I, shame-faced, followed her lead to make sure she didn't lose her own ration on my account. And so the sawing got done, all because of Riva, my friend and savior. Never once did she complain about me, except perhaps to her mother, and even that she had to do in secret, because we all lived in one room—she and her mother, me and mine. Somehow she put up with our friendship and even seemed to take pride in it. At the end of the day we'd head home along the path—Riva in front with her ax stuck into her belt and the saw over her shoulder, me behind with a runny nose and an armload of kindling. Our mothers would be anxiously awaiting us breadwinners. "You poor things!" they'd cry. "Slaving all day in the forest!" They'd help us take off our frozen clothes and hurry the hot soup to the table.

❧ ❧ ❧

Who was Riva and how did I get to know her? Even to ask such a question is to acknowledge that Riva was not one of us, not from Zgurița but from outside. We met for the first time in Kipryushka, and after that we stuck together for quite a while. Eventually we got fed up with each other and raised no objections when the boss assigned us to different work stations, but that was a few years later. At first, during our honeymoon period, Riva and her mother, Madam Gleyzer, as she was known, hung on our every word and tried to do everything we did. Having come from a village without any other Jews called Șuri, near Drochia, where we'd been loaded into the railroad cars, they knew little about Jewish customs. They'd made the terrible journey to Siberia among their non-Jewish neighbors. On the barge, though, quick-witted Madam Gleyzer spotted us Jews from Zgurița, and as we were all getting off in Kipryushka, she took advantage of the general confusion to get some of her Moldovan acquaintances to carry her trunk over to our area in exchange for a few coins. The two women followed, arms full of bundles and eyes full of tears.

"I've lived all my life with *goyim*," Madam Gleyzer announced to the crowd. "I want to spend the rest of my life with Jews."

Well put, I thought. And indeed, people began to move over to free up space, while my mother urged them on in her usual forceful way. "Since when do we have reserved seats here in Siberia?" she said. "There's plenty of room." She motioned to the two women. "Make yourselves comfortable," she said, "and may the Lord remember us and deliver us from bondage, *bimheyre beyemeynu*, speedily in our days, amen."

"Amen," Madam Glazer repeated after her, as if sealing an agreement. She kept repeating the word, as if marveling over her good fortune in attaching herself and her daughter to us. She singled out my mother and me and stuck to us like glue.

So my relationship with Riva began. It was fine with me, and as for Riva ... most of the time she went around in a daze while her poor mother fussed over her and did everything she could to cheer her up. At least she'd provided her with a decent girlfriend.

What was Riva's problem? A great tragedy had occurred, one that was difficult for a nineteen-year-old girl to handle. It turned out we'd heard something about it at the very beginning, back at the station in Drochia, before the train began moving, when we were "taking our seats" in the railroad cars—that is, grabbing a spot on the floor. Don't think there was no pushing or shoving, though at first people tried to affect a modicum of respect for the elders and other esteemed townspeople. We stayed in Drochia for twenty-four hours while the transport was being arranged, and all that time the crowd was abuzz with rumors that there was a girl who kept fainting, a young woman who was supposed to be married the day after tomorrow.

Really, the day after tomorrow? Yes, the call to the Torah was on Shabbos and the wedding was going to be the day after tomorrow. Quite a wedding, too! They'd hired the hall and the musicians in Bălţi months ago, and the baking and all the other preparations had been going on for weeks. But then those devils—worse than devils, really. At least you can bargain with the devil, but with these thugs … Believe me, they tried bargaining. Her father fell at their feet and begged for mercy. With the Angel of Death you should beg, but with them? The poor man pleaded with them to postpone the order for three days so he could lead his child to the wedding canopy. "After that you can do whatever you want," he said. "Go ahead, chop my head off!"

Well, canopy-shmanopy, they paid no attention, but what was this about chopping off his head? *That* smacked of anti-Sovietism, and that was too much. "Any more bourgeois backtalk out of you and you'll lose your head for real," and they started shoving him and throwing things. "*Davay, davay,* get moving!" They carried him out on a stretcher.

Oy, a man is stronger than iron!

A few weeks later, at a stop farther along the way, I caught sight of the girl, but at the time I had no idea she was the same unfortunate bride we'd been talking about back in Drochia. That day our train was driven onto a siding, the bars were removed from the doors, and we were released for a few hours into an open field. Oh, the fresh air and the sweet-smelling grass! People balanced pots on a couple of stones and boiled what they could—mostly plain water. One woman had managed to get hold of some cornmeal and make a *mamaliga*. With tears in her eyes, she was begging her daughter to try some. I watched this scene from a distance, my mouth watering, unable to imagine how anyone in our situation could be miserable enough to turn down such a hot, tasty meal.

How could I know that this girl and I would soon be living together, working together, sharing secrets?

✦ ✦ ✦

Apparently Riva cried out all her tears during the journey to Siberia. By the time we arrived she was silent. She worked and didn't talk. Not a word out of her mouth. On Sundays, though, our day of rest, she would open her trunk, sit down on a little stool, and with heartrending tenderness lift out, one at a time, all the gifts she'd received for the engagement and the wedding. She'd examine each item in turn, carefully running her fingers over the candlesticks, the silverware, the embroidered tablecloths, the vases, the beautiful china. She suffered especially over a certain tray. It was a round one, for cakes, made in the latest style, with a lacy silver base, a garland of flowers on the surface, and in the center a portrait of the happy couple, Riva and her groom, with their heads together. Whenever she picked up the tray, her mother would stand by with a damp towel to use as a compress if necessary.

At first I felt great sympathy for Riva. I would see her trembling lips and my heart would ache for her. Then I got tired of the scenes with the trunk, and when I saw Madam Gleyzer come running with the towel, I would roll over in bed, turn my face to the wall, and immerse myself in my geography book, the only book I'd been able to find on the site, which I was using to teach myself Russian. Later on, the business with the trunk began to grate on my nerves. One Sunday, the weather was so cold that you could hear the bark cracking on the trees, and I couldn't have been more miserable. A big boil on my back had just popped, a carbuncle, which hurt worse than a toothache, and nothing would help—not bandages, not warm dressings, not even the soothing touch of my mother's soft hands. That day I couldn't bear it any longer. I lost my temper and let loose at her, perhaps more harshly than I should have.

"What, Riva?" I spat. "You think you're the only one who's miserable? You think nobody else is suffering? Nobody else had to give up anything? Nobody else had to leave anything behind? Believe me, Riva, the rest of us have it just as bad as you—just as bad."

Riva turned and looked at me as if she were trying to decide whether I had actually spoken these words or whether she'd only imagined them. Quickly she put everything back in the trunk and slammed it shut.

A black cat had run between us. Afterwards I tried to take back what I'd said, but I only made things worse.

❖ ❖ ❖

Riva was strange. She wasn't exactly eccentric, but … today we might say she had a complex. Maybe the problem was that she was smart—too smart, perhaps. She was always thinking about things—above all about herself. Once, for example, she said to me something like this: "Look at the two of us. I'm a little village girl who knows how to whitewash a wall so you can't see a single brush mark when I'm done—but when I try to write a letter to my fiancé, I have to do it over ten times, with my stomach tied up in knots. Or take the way you talk. It sounds like Yiddish, but I can't always understand what you're saying."

"Ay, Riva," I replied, "it doesn't matter. Don't make such a crease in your yarmulke."

"That's exactly what I'm talking about!" she said. "What does a yarmulke have to do with anything, and why shouldn't I make a crease in it?"

I laughed so hard my eyes filled with tears. Looking at me, Riva started laughing too, stifling her giggles the way she did, with her hand over her mouth.

Another time—this, too, was before my outburst with the trunk—we'd roasted two potatoes in the embers of the fire that Riva was a world specialist at lighting, even when the snow was knee-deep. We were in a good mood. That day we'd been blessed with a tree so easy that the saw went through like butter. All our wood was sawed and chopped, and the only thing we had left to do was to build our stack, so we were allowing ourselves a break. Suddenly Riva began to unburden herself about her fiancé.

"I wonder whether Volodya is still alive," she said. "And if he is, I wonder if he'll come looking for me so we can get married."

"What are you saying, Riva?" I said. "You were engaged, so you must have been in love."

"Of course I was in love," she answered. "I'm still in love. I'm crazy about him. At night when I can't sleep, I miss him so much I'm afraid I'm losing my mind. But it's not me I'm wondering about, it's him. You don't know how handsome he is—tall, with muscles and gorgeous eyes, and his hair—well, you've seen his picture."

"You don't look so shabby yourself," I said.

"I know," she said. "I may not be ugly or stupid or lazy or bad or whatever you just said, shabby, and besides, my father promised him a big dowry. But that's all gone now. So what's the chance he's going to come looking for me?

Look at the fire—it burns and it burns and then it goes out
… The worst is when I remember my father, so clever, so
full of life, such a decent man, groveling at their feet, and
all because of me! Oh, it drives me wild."

Given that conversation, you can see why it was so
cruel of me to attack Riva that Sunday. I was the one she'd
entrusted with her most precious secrets, the only one to
whom she'd opened her heart. And yet I was the one who
rubbed salt in her wounds. I couldn't forgive myself. Nor
did she forgive me. She would have had to be an angel—
or at least be my mother, who could always find something in my favor when I offended her. But Riva was not
my mother or even my sister, and she was no angel. She
wasn't inclined to make allowances for my suffering, and
she took it very hard when I slapped her in the face the
way I did that day. Apparently she'd thought highly of me
and expected better. She was very disappointed.

Not long after, I softened my heart and tried to make
up with her.

"Riva," I said, "it's enough already. I feel terrible about
what I said—I can't even express how bad I feel. As they
say, an ox may have a long tongue, but it can't blow a
shofar."

She shot me an angry look. "Leave me alone with your
Hebrew talk," she said.

"If that's Hebrew talk," I said, "then I'm a rabbi's wife."

That was the end of our friendship.

❖ ❖ ❖

And now for how she paid me back. Many years later—at
least twenty years, maybe more—we met one more time.
She and her husband came to Kishinev from Samarkand,

where they'd settled after the liberation. She wasn't with Volodya. After her mother died, she'd married a man from Zgurița, a deportee like us, of course. They were in town to see his friends, and she took the opportunity to visit me. By then we were well into our forties, with quite a bit of gray hair and fine lines in the corners of our eyes. Our meeting was very touching; we laughed and cried as one does on such occasions. Before leaving, all of a sudden she asked a question. "So," she said, "I see things are going well with you, but what about—what about the other things?"

"What other things?" I said.

"I mean …" She hesitated. "I mean … besides your family and your job. I mean"—all at once she found her tongue—"what about your writing, about getting published? If I remember correctly, you used to dream about—didn't you want something more?"

I looked at her with the same expression she'd fixed on me in front of the open trunk, as if I were trying to decide whether quiet Riva had truly spoken these words or whether I'd just imagined she had.

Riva returned my gaze with a thin smile and quickly took her leave. She looked quite pleased with herself.

A SEDER IN THE TAIGA

It was the only time in my life when everyone at the Passover table was thinking only about the Haggadah, not the matzo balls—perhaps because there wasn't a whiff of a matzo ball to be found.

That year in Siberia, spring arrived a few weeks earlier than expected. Here and there, the Ob began to thaw. We had to stop crossing the river by sled, and even walking on the ice became risky, so we stayed home and waited to be able to make it over by boat. This waiting was no small problem. Of course we were accustomed to waiting, but it's one thing to wait when you're getting your daily bread ration or have a few potatoes, beets, or turnips on hand—and quite another when your cupboard is completely bare, and the few "prosperous" Siberians in the area, the old-time settlers, can't be persuaded to part with the smallest crumb, no matter what you offer. Everyone's reserves were running low. People wouldn't risk taking food out of their own mouths for all the money in the world.

As if that weren't enough, God sent us yet another plague—not one from the Haggadah but a Siberian one. The heavy layers of snow that had built up during the long winter caused the chimney of the bakery in Krasny Yar to collapse. Alas, this was the only large-scale bakery in the area. It provided bread to villages and settlements for miles around. What were we to do? Three times a day, we gobbled down whatever meager nourishment we could put our hands on. We gathered mushrooms in the forest and ate them with the wild garlic the Siberians called *kolba*, and before we'd swallowed the last spoonful we were hungry again.

Two weeks passed like this, and then came word from Krasny Yar, where the village council and our commandant were located, saying that if we sent two strong young men with sleds, they would give us the sacks of flour we were owed for the two weeks. After that ... God willing, the bakery would soon be back in operation.

The entire district turned out to send off the expedition. Everyone had a suggestion, a word of advice, a blessing. The journey would be difficult, as the road was not smooth but full of puddles, so that even empty sleds were hard to move. A week passed before we saw them come crawling back, inching along with the help of those who'd been sent to meet them.

In this way the Lord provided us with matzo for Passover. The non-Jews made potato dumplings they called *kletsky*, as well as *zatirukha*, a thin potato soup, and since it was the day before Passover, the Jewish women used our portion to bake matzo.

Baking matzo—how impressive that sounds. It wasn't egg matzo, and it certainly wasn't made according to the traditional rules. The dough kept falling apart under the rolling pin, and the matzos came out tiny, each no bigger than a yawn, but they were matzos all the same. Also, they were the color of clay. Nonetheless, they were very tasty. Where is it written that matzos must be crisp and pale? Our matzos certainly filled the bill for a Siberian "bread of affliction."

All the Jewish families from our section and the one next to ours came to the seder, and there was matzo for everyone. My mother led the ceremony. Since we had no Haggadahs, she proposed that we celebrate the seder in a new way. Year after year, she said, we'd conducted the seder according to the rules laid down by the scholars of old, but this year, by necessity, we'd add our own twist. We would not ask the Four Questions, first of all because there was no one to ask them of, and second because once we began asking we wouldn't be done till morning. Our questions weren't actually questions anyway, they were complaints, directed at God. For example, why on this day do we not eat leavened bread? Very simple. Because the bakery in Krasny Yar isn't operating. And *maror*? We have more bitter herbs than we need; we've all eaten *kolba* till we're green in the face. As for dipping, we're drowning in a sea of tears, and when it comes to reclining instead of sitting upright, we're reclining, all right—up to our necks in the middle of nowhere.

We were slaves in Egypt, my mother said, and today we're slaves of Stalin, exiled to hard labor in the Siberian taiga, without rights and without the slightest hope of rescue.

Why, my mother continued, should we listen to what Eliezer said thousands of years ago about the exodus from Egypt, or quote from the words of Reb Berl or Reb Shmerl, when right here at the table, Aunt Gitl and Madam Gleyzer, Madam Gurevits and Sonya Shmukler, Sheyndl Gelman and Madam Shvartsman, can tell us about how their homes were destroyed in the dark of night and their families torn asunder without a why or wherefore? Let each of us tell how we used to live in our little towns, upholding our Jewish traditions and our humanity, caring for the poor, distributing challah for Shabbos and matzos for Passover, providing dowries to needy brides and aiding the destitute. Yet even so, the Lord sent His messenger to condemn us to wander and suffer in the Siberian taiga.

If we had been exiled and not separated from the men—*dayenu!* That would have been misery enough! But no, the cup of suffering had to be drained to the very dregs. Our men had to be separated from us and sent to the slave labor camps in the Urals, while we women and children were condemned to die in the taiga.

Our sins, my mother said, must have been great indeed to cause the Lord to pour out His wrath upon us. Great indeed to cause Him to send down the plagues upon us rather than upon our oppressors. And speaking of wrath, why, Lord, are You always full of wrath, and why must You always be visiting Your wrath on someone else? After all, it was You who created the world that turned out the way it did. You have only Yourself to blame.

Everyone agreed. We all contributed our share to the unwritten Siberian Haggadah, until the hour grew late, and we noticed the seder plate sitting on the table like a poor bride dressed in borrowed finery. A boiled potato scrounged up from somewhere, a bone from God-knows-what animal, a pine cone in place of an egg, berries instead of *charoses*, and a big heap of *maror—kolba*, of course. Everyone at the table shared in the bounty, we said a blessing, and the meal was served. We finished up with strong tea brewed from dried lingonberry leaves, and then we sang. We put our own special stamp on the songs. We ended the "Who knows one?" song partway through, right after the Four Matriarchs, so as to give pride of place to the "*Khad-gadye*," the song in which the cat devours the goat, the dog bites the cat, the stick beats the dog, and so on and so on—one big outpouring of pain and suffering without any attempt to make peace, just killing and burning and devouring on all sides, until finally the Angel of Death kills the slaughterer, at which point God finally realizes that things have gone too far and steps in to end the massacre.

Isn't it remarkable, my mother said, what people can take pleasure in, what they can believe in, in times of need? We tell ourselves a terrible story, we slap on a happy ending—and praised be the Lord, *leoylem-vo'ed*, forever. We repeat the story generation after generation and cling like drowning people to the hope that the same God who led our forefathers out of Egypt will also rescue us from here, *bimheyre beyemeynu*, speedily in our days, amen!

None of us wanted to think that this seder might be our last. But by the next year, my mother was no longer alive, and other women from our town of Zgurița had also died before their time. They lie buried in the Siberian earth for eternity. We never had any more matzos, whether miraculous ones or not, and never again did we feel a desire to celebrate another seder in Siberia.

ON THE LANDING

Krivosheino, the regional center, sat on the Ob River, on the other shore, far to the north. The river was frozen for more than half the year, so it was possible to get there by sleigh, but most people went on foot, pulling little sleds behind them. For two months of the year—October, when the ice was beginning to form, and May, when it was breaking up—you could neither ride nor walk; then you stayed home. In the summer you could take the steamer that connected the river towns of the Narym region: Krasny Yar, Kipryushka, Nikol'skoye, Krivosheino, Molchanovo, and so on, all the way to Kolpashevo and beyond. The boat crept along like a tortoise and had no established schedule—it came when it came. Depending on your luck, you could wait for twenty-four hours, or for two days or three or more. And where did you spend those three days? On the landing, of course: a trampled patch of earth with a sign, a flag mounted on a pole, and a massive piling where the boat would tie up. There you could sit down, or even stretch out on the ground, if you weren't afraid of mosquitoes, ticks, or assorted other biting and crawling insects. If you wanted something to eat, you could help yourself to whatever you'd brought with you. Otherwise, you could starve to death on the landing and no one would bat an eye.

Ester had brought food. Besides having to wait for the boat, she knew that no one would be waiting for her in Krivosheino with a good meal; she'd be hungry by the time she got where she was going. Nothing would hold her back, though. This time she'd decided once and for all to escape from the forest. She wasn't going to think about what would happen at the other end. In her sack she had some boiled potatoes, two turnips, and three days' worth of bread rations, divided into slices to help keep her hands off the share for the next meal. She had some salt, too, tied up in a scrap of white cloth. She had to stick with the plan to the end, she kept telling herself, or else there would be no end to her suffering. It was hard to say how she'd come up with the plan. It had occurred to her out of the blue, really. Back at the base, she'd happened to hear that the region's annual teacher conference was coming up in Krivosheino. A longing had come upon her, a gnawing nostalgia. She yearned to spend even a day among those lucky teachers, to sit in the hall listening to presentations, no matter what they were about. How long had it been since she was seated proudly on stage, a member of the board, the envy of everyone in the room? God, what has become of me, she asked herself. A lump formed in her throat, and suddenly the idea came that she must seize this opportunity no matter the cost. Nothing ventured, nothing gained. Maybe the plan wouldn't succeed, but as the slogan had it, "dead or Red!"—she had to try. Among the papers she'd hastily packed and brought with her to Siberia was a certificate stating that she was a village teacher. With luck, maybe they wouldn't look too closely, wouldn't notice the certificate was from Moldova, and would let her onto the boat. And what do you know? That's exactly what happened. Holding the paper stamped by the ministry of education, she was taken for a peasant girl, a teacher from one of the local farming communities, and was waved onto the boat without ado—*davay, davay,* hurry up, get on, we're late.

And that would have been the end of the tale, if not for the most important part of the story, which happened earlier, on the landing. So let's back up.

Tired from her long walk, Ester had sat down on the riverbank, taken off her heavy sandals and put her feet in the river. Bliss! The water cooled her burning feet and drained the weariness from her limbs. She sat and sat; she couldn't get enough. Then she furtively wrapped up the sandals, put them in her sack, and pulled out her shoes. Now that she was among people, she needed to look like a person. She was in no hurry to eat. That morning she'd had a double portion of soup. In return for a pink hair ribbon, the cook had scooped up two whole ladles from the bottom of the pot, the thick part. She'd filled herself up. But since then a whole day had passed, and quite a day at that. She'd walked as fast as she could—it would be just her luck if the boat came today and she arrived too late, in time to see it recede into the distance, wagging its tail as it disappeared out of sight. She'd pushed herself to the limit, not permitting herself a moment's rest. So it wasn't that she wasn't hungry—she was always hungry—but she knew there would be no food tomorrow. Best to make do now with a slice of bread and a little water from the river, and save the potatoes for later.

Meanwhile, night fell, and those who were waiting on the landing, ten or twelve of them, built a fire to protect against the swarms of mosquitoes eager to take up a collection from the assembly. She had no choice but to move closer to the fire herself, and that was when she saw him. He was standing on the other side of the fire, directly across from her, in the riding breeches they all wore, the big belt buckle, and the familiar NKVD cap. Ester froze and thought she might pass out. So—you escape from hell and here's the devil in your face. It was none other than Shapovalov, the camp commandant who supervised the deportees who worked in the forest chemical works. What could be worse? Shapovalov was about thirty years old and lived in Krasny Yar. Only rarely did he show up at the site. Instead he had his minions, who served as his guard dogs, keeping an eye on every move. Every so often he paid a short visit to see and be seen. It was said that he wasn't a bad guy, but to the prisoners he was not a guy at all, good or bad, but always the commandant. Even if you weren't afraid of the man himself, the blue cap with the red stripe and the star in front still made you tremble. That cap and those trousers struck terror in the hearts of everyone in the forest.

To this day, Ester doesn't know whether he didn't see her, or whether he just pretended not to see. It wasn't a question of recognizing her personally. To him, she was just one of the masses. But all the deportees were easy to identify by their tattered clothes and by how intent they were on hiding. Their scarves were always pulled down low on their foreheads, their eyes full of fear. The deportees had good reason to be afraid. Their fates were in his hands. In this instance, he could decide whether Ester got on the boat to Krivosheino or went back to the forest.

✦ ✦ ✦

He didn't even glance in her direction, but the exaggerated way he seemed to be avoiding her made Ester suspect that he'd seen her. What to do? She lowered her eyes. It's in God's hands, she told herself. Every minute felt like an eternity. She turned her head away, then worried that she would attract his attention by looking as if she were trying to hide, so she turned back to the fire, staring straight ahead and pinching herself with her hands in her pockets. Lord, how much longer? A minute passed, then another, ten more. He seemed to be playing a game of cat and mouse, certain that his victim wouldn't escape. It was not easy being a mouse, even in an imaginary game. She broke into a cold sweat.

The game lasted so long that she found herself beginning to relax. If he were planning to punish her, surely he wouldn't have let things go on so long. He would have thrown her out right away. Letting it go was a sign ... a sign of something, even if she couldn't figure out what. A flicker of hope began to glow. Maybe he wasn't going to turn her in after all. The boat was coming—please God!

The commandant was not alone. With him was someone else, also from the NKVD but evidently of lower rank—the commandant called him Sashka, and this Sashka never opened his mouth, only listened and smiled, while his superior never stopped talking. No doubt Shapovalov felt it was beneath his dignity to have to wait on this muddy landing with ordinary people. He was laughing and talking loudly, probably hoping people would notice that he was no regular fellow but a big-shot official. When his initial supply of stories had run out, he started talking about carrots. He told Sashka, who was standing by the fire not far from Ester, that he had never eaten a carrot in his life and never would, not for all the money in the world. He loathed carrots and wouldn't let them pass his lips, not raw, not boiled, not even baked the way everyone loved them. It drove his mother crazy, but he couldn't stand to look at them. It was a perfect boast. Refusing to eat a carrot—what better proof that he was living the good life?

Meanwhile he was tearing open a bag of cookies, round, plump ones like the spice cookies from back home. He ate one and playfully tossed a second to Sashka over the fire, then a third. Whenever Sashka made a catch, the two of them laughed uproariously. Then one of the cookies fell and rolled close to Ester. Sashka shrugged—it wasn't worth bending down. There lay the cookie, suddenly the center of the universe. Ester forgot all about the commandant. All she could think was that someone else would see the cookie and pick it up. Lifting her eyes as if to study the stars, she edged over and gently covered the cookie with her foot, not crushing it but nudging it deeper into the grass. A little later, when it seemed no one was looking, she picked it up, brushed it off, and gobbled it down, her heart weeping with every bite.

Did he witness her in her moment of degradation? Did he drop the cookie at her feet on purpose to humiliate her? To this day, Ester does not know.

MONA BUBBE

Everyone in the city knew her, but none of us knew her real name. No one knew where she came from or who she really was—Jewish? Christian?—but we accepted her anyway, along with her peculiar name. Someone had dubbed her "Mona Bubbe" behind her back, and everyone called her that as if there was nothing strange about it, because ... well, because in truth she didn't matter much to any of us.

❖ ❖ ❖

In the first years after the war, Jews began returning from the evacuation. First we wept over the ashes of our ruined towns, and then we moved to the cities and looked for a place to live—a corner, a room under a leaky roof, anywhere we could settle down and unpack our troubles.

New to the big city, we were hungry for something familiar to nourish our souls, something to call our own. We
were overjoyed when we ran into Khatskl, the gaunt,
towering prophet who seemed to have been sent straight
from Heaven to lift our spirits and relieve our loneliness.
Khatskl was delighted with us, too. So long as we gathered
around and kept listening, he didn't care who we were.
Often enough he forgot we were there and addressed
himself directly to the Lord of the Universe. Day and
night, he went around in a shapeless overcoat three sizes
too big, clasping an open book to his chest like the Ten
Commandments. We started thinking of him as a kind of
Moses, though unlike Moses he didn't stutter—in fact, his
tongue was as sharp as a knife.

Our Khatskl always orated in Hebrew, and never in
a side street but always in the center of town, or sometimes in the park where we used to stroll in the evenings
in search of the latest gossip. A crowd would form, some
admiring, others shaking their heads over the crazy fool.
Some worried that the man's recklessness would get him
into big trouble. They begged him to watch his step, stop
his flapping and jabbering. But it wasn't easy to reason with
him. He believed he was God's messenger. It was up to him
to create peace and unity in the world, to persuade the lost
flock to stop following the false messiah—that is, the Soviet
regime. Yes, he went that far. Fortunately, even among us
Jews, hardly anyone could understand what he was talking
about. Most of us considered him a harmless lunatic. But
the secret police had people who specialized in such types.
They concluded that this Khatskl with the baggy coat was
only pretending to be a madman. He might look like a disturbed person, but that was only a mask. In fact he was

an American agent, an anti-Soviet propagandist. In short order he was whisked away, and no trace remained of the prophet with the giant coat and the holy book. Now the streets were deserted, especially in the evenings.

It took a while for Mona Bubbe to show up. Why "Mona Bubbe"? Well, why not? First of all, she was a woman, so she needed a woman's name. And, whenever she thought someone was making fun of her, she'd flash her eyes and gnash her teeth like a *baba*, a witch. Your blood would curdle. But at the same time you'd see a curious smile on her lips, just like the Mona Lisa. So some joker came up with the name Mona Baba, a combination of beauty and hag that was about as bizarre as she was. Since people were pretty sure she was a Jew, it didn't take long for her to become Mona Bubbe. The Jewish word for "grandma" gave her a kind of protection, as if our community were watching over her. In fact, she was a minor character who would never take the place of Khatskl the prophet in our hearts—but still, she was better than nothing.

✦ ✦ ✦

After the completion of "Komsomol Lake" and the splendid tree-lined path that surrounded it, another site to the south was designated for an impressive stairway with columns, fountains, and new plantings. The whole area was grandly dubbed the "Summer Garden," just like in Leningrad. There were halls where various games were played, a movie theater, and an open-air stage. All in all, it was a magnificent city project that provided the starving population with cultural activities to consume along with our miserable crusts of postwar bread.

At first people went down to the park in droves to breathe the fresh air and enjoy performances by the philharmonic. Later, when we had a little butter or sausage to go with our bread, we went less often, especially on weekdays, and we skipped the free concerts. Most of the benches in front of the stage sat empty, in spite of the hardworking musicians all dressed up in their tuxedos with flowers in their lapels. They were required to play, whether or not anyone was listening. The whole thing was painful for them—artists don't like sawing away for no applause. But eventually they adjusted and even came to find the situation somewhat amusing, especially since in fact not all the benches were unoccupied. Every day, their devoted listener, the one and only Mona Bubbe, took her place in the front row.

Who knows? Maybe the concerts became part of her daily routine for no particular reason, or maybe she was a classical music fan. In any event, she never missed a concert. Every day the musicians placed a white flower on her seat, matching the ones in their buttonholes, and waited for her before starting to play.

As befitted a lady entering a concert hall, Mona Bubbe arrived dressed to the nines, every detail reflecting her personal sense of style. Over a white blouse she wore a checkered jacket adorned with tucks and pleats. A round black hat perched on top of her head and a checkered ribbon tangled fetchingly in her long, loose hair. Her white gloves were cheap but spotless, and she carried a black purse with the kind of fringe that was fashionable about fifty years ago.

What stood out most, though, wasn't her clothing. The poor woman really went to town with her makeup. She

covered her moon face with a thick layer of powder, out-
lined her eyes with coal-black pencil, and smeared cheap
red lipstick like a clown's over her lips. People couldn't
stop staring at her, but none of us said anything. No one
wanted to get involved—not that she would have paid
attention anyway.

On the bandstand, none of it mattered. When the musicians saw her coming, they'd strike up a march. She'd lower
her eyes coquettishly, and the corners of her painted lips
would turn up with pleasure. She'd sniff at her flower, take
her seat, and gracefully signal that she was ready to listen.

Then the concert would begin. Fool or not, Mona
Bubbe knew exactly how to behave when she felt accepted
rather than pushed away. What an honor it was to be
entertained by such renowned virtuosos! When it came
time to applaud, she pulled off her gloves and made as
much noise as she could in the empty space. Which side
got more out of the encounter—she or the ensemble—
was an open question.

So a year passed, then another. As the violinists grew
older, they were not replaced. Most of the players were
Jews, though some Moldovans, onetime wedding musicians, could also be found among the basses, the big
horns, and maybe the cymbals and the kettledrums.

Our Mona Bubbe wasn't getting any younger either. A
distinct web of wrinkles could be seen around her mouth,
even under the thick layer of powder.

❖ ❖ ❖

One day when Mona Bubbe arrived in the park, a violin-
ist and a cellist were missing. She noticed right away but

didn't feel she had the right to ask, so she said nothing. After the concert she lingered by the gate but still couldn't bring herself to approach anyone. She went home upset and on edge. Not long after, two more cellists and the principal clarinetist disappeared. Mona Bubbe nearly fell ill. She stopped going to the park. Let them manage without her. By the time she learned the whole story, it was too late. Now, in the evenings, the bandstand in the Summer Garden stood empty, except for the boys who strutted around on the stage before going to the cinema.

Mona Bubbe had lost her anchor. All of her beloved musicians were leaving the country. She couldn't begin to understand why. It felt like a personal blow. How could they abandon her after all her years of devotion? She took to snarling and spouting profanities in the streets again, then went back to the Summer Garden, hoping for news. It was unbelievable that they would run off without even saying goodbye. She ached, she agonized, and then she made up her mind.

On a Wednesday, Mona Bubbe screwed up her courage and set off for the train station. The platform was jammed—so many traitors all in one place! Trembling, she kept close to the wall. She knew that when people were in a festive mood they tended to pay more attention to her. Best to stay safely out of sight.

Everything was in such an uproar that at first no one even noticed the train pulling in on platform one. Then the real crush began. People screamed and hollered and climbed on top of one another to toss their luggage through the windows. Why such a rush, Mona Bubbe wondered sourly. Was life here so unbearable—even with the philharmonic and the Summer Garden? What was the matter with them all? Then, suddenly, three violinists caught her eye. They were already on the train, standing at the window and saying goodbye to their companions. Mona Bubbe felt faint. She lowered her eyes. Better not to look, not to see the loathsome world that had forgotten her so easily, abandoned her so casually to the likes of drunken Vaska, wobbling and tottering with the cymbals in his hands. Who now would welcome her to the park with a march? Where would she find refuge? Choking back tears, she turned her face to the wall. It was then that they recognized her by the ribbon in her long hair. Mona Bubbe—here, for them! Deeply moved, they waved and smiled, but she wasn't looking.

"What's her name?" one of them asked the others.

"You know—Mona Bubbe!"

"Not that—her real name!"

No one knew.

"Try it—maybe she'll answer."

"Mona Bubbe!" Their voices rang out on the platform.

She didn't turn. And when a young man nearby tapped her on the shoulder, she only bared her teeth and shoved him away.

"You crazy thing, what are you hitting me for? Can't you hear them?" He pointed at the train. She turned then and saw the three violinists beaming and waving goodbye.

Everyone on the platform was gawking at her. Mona Bubbe lifted her head and seemed about to speak, but instead her face twisted. The tears that were caught in her throat spilled out over her cheeks, mingling together the moon-white of her face, her coal-black eyes, and the wine-dark red of her lips.

BY THE LIGHT OF THE MOON

Try taking apart a head of cauliflower, and you'll see right away that every part, no matter how small, is itself a head of cauliflower, with the same type of stalk, the same curly little head, the same smell, the same taste. This is how it was in Bessarabia, the place that was once our home but is now no more. The cities and towns were so much alike, it was as if they'd been born of the same mother. Even in the tiniest town you could find everything a Jewish community needed: a rabbi, a judge, a mohel—and more kosher butchers and study houses than you could count.

Our own town was Zgurița. Over the years I've come to think of it as what in modern times might be called "Greater Zgurița," because it served Jewish families in the surrounding villages—Zgura, Nicorești, Popeștii, and so on. In these villages, Jews lived among Moldovan farmers and ran the inns and mills owned by the aristocrats. But although they earned their living in the villages, spiritually they belonged to the town. From birth to burial, they made use of the Jewish institutions in Zgurița and helped pay for their upkeep. In its last decade, Greater Zgurița was home to a splendid "Temple of Culture." Don't be surprised—it was nothing like today's Temples of Culture (no offense intended to these, of course). Our Temple of Culture was the Tarbut School, our secondary school, our pride and joy. To this day, if you track down any of the sons and daughters of Zgurița, now scattered to the four corners of the earth, and ask them what the town was best known for, every one of them without fail will say the Tarbut School. Whether you'd ever been a student at the school, or the parent of one, made no difference—the school belonged to us all. It was ours, built with love, with our own hands, right next to another important building—the Sharey Tsiyon synagogue.

The close proximity of the two buildings was meant to embody the words of the *Ki Mitzion* prayer, which is sung when the Torah is removed from the ark in the synagogue: "From here shall go forth the law"—learning and wisdom shall emanate from this place.

The community scrimped and saved and sacrificed to build this magnificent temple of learning. And then came the Lord with a fiery tempest that annihilated the Jews.

The town was no more. Where the finest houses had stood—nothing but craters of ash. Here and there, the conflagration missed a house or two, leaving traces that made it impossible to deny that Jewish life had once flowered in these parts. Who can understand God's plan, His ways of punishing one and sparing another?

Among the few buildings that miraculously remained intact after the great destruction were the synagogue and the school. They stand there still—upon their foundations, but no longer upon the pedestals we put them on. They've lost their splendor, their power to awe and inspire. Alas, the synagogue is now a grain warehouse, the Tarbut School an ordinary middle school. The blessing that used to close the Sabbath, separating the sacred from the profane, is long since forgotten in the town. Today the sacred is no more; only the profane remains. Time passes unmarked by the Jewish calendar, the age-old order that had ruled the days and weeks and months of the year from generation to generation.

Now alien customs and unfamiliar ways hold sway in the town. In the evenings, in place of the old blessings is only heartache, an unseen tear. But when the moon is full, something surprising occurs. Shadows reach out to embrace one another. The moon looks down and pricks up her ears. What's going on down there? The moon strains to listen. Surely these are not the traditional prayers. The moon grows pale, then paler, until she begins to understand: no, the sounds emanating from below are not from the prayer book, not meant in her honor. Instead, the shadow of the Sharey Tsiyon synagogue has reached out to touch the Tarbut School. By the light of the moon, the synagogue is caressing her younger sister, soothing her with tales of long ago.

THE IRONY OF FATE

Hersh Levinzon was almost eighty years old when he learned one day that under Soviet law he and Ester were not legally married, which meant he wasn't entitled to the extra ten percent in pension money he'd been expecting.

"May it happen to my enemies!" he grumbled over and over to Avrom, as if his son were to blame for the torments visited upon him. It wasn't the measly rubles but the principle of the thing. "What do they mean, not legal? What are we, boyfriend and girlfriend? That would make you a bastard, my son, and the same with your brother and sister—all bastards, ha? But what can you expect from a country that puts Grishka the Thief on a stone horse?"

Avrom struggled not to smile. This was a reference to the grand memorial in Kishinev in honor of Grigory Kotovsky, the great Soviet hero, remembered by old inhabitants of Bessarabia as a simple horse thief in his youth. Avrom didn't dare laugh at his father, not to his face. His brother Shmulik would have made some crack at the expense of the old man, but not Avrom, the first-born, the big shot, the head of household in the spacious apartment where his parents were living out their old age in dignity. Avrom refrained from laughing both out of respect and also out of fear that too much excitement would be bad for his father's weak heart.

People marveled at Avrom's closeness to his parents and couldn't understand why such a devoted son would allow his elderly father to go to work just for the extra cash. Here he was, Avrom Levinzon, director of central optical production, in charge of supplying all of Moldova with eyeglasses and everything connected with eyeglasses. With his access to goodies that other people couldn't even dream of, did he really need the paltry wages his father earned as a cashier in a pharmacy? Avrom knew what people were whispering behind his back, but decided he didn't owe anyone an explanation and did what he thought best. It worked out well. Immediately after returning from the evacuation, he'd used his connections with the phar-macy manager to secure the position for his father. At that time, what mattered most was not the salary but the ration cards that employees received for themselves and their family members. Hersh Levinzon, then in his early sixties, was glad for the job. "I don't want to depend on the chil-dren for room and board," he said. "I don't want to have to come to them for every little thing." He rolled up his sleeves and showed the lazybones at the pharmacy what work looked like, what doing your duty was all about.

Anyone unfamiliar with the way the economy func-tioned in the Soviet Union will find it difficult to grasp the essence of that "ingenious" system. Rubles by the millions disappeared into thin air, looted and plundered without the slightest pang, but coins were counted meticulously, to the point of madness. The system was especially evident at the pharmacies, where medications were literally sold by the kopek. In those years in Russia there were no calculators. The cashiers did their figuring in a primitive fashion, jotting down all the monies they collected in the course of a shift on long sheets of paper. A bottle of mouthwash for three kopeks, for example, was written as 0-03, and a tin of ointment for five kopeks was 0-05—all in one long column. At the end of each shift the columns were totaled up and the final sum squared with the cash in the till. Most cashiers at that time used an abacus, a counting frame with movable beads, which was considered a big step forward on the road to Progressive Mechanization. Hersh Levinzon didn't believe in such "modernizations." In his view, they dulled the mind to the point where a person couldn't add two plus two on his own. He stuck with the tried and true—adding figures in his head. You could hear his lips whispering quick-quick-quick, like nuts rolling down a hill, and before you knew it he had the balance. Not once had he been caught in a mistake. Everyone in the pharmacy was in awe. Outwardly indifferent to praise but secretly pleased, the old man would calmly write down the final figure, sign the account with a flourish, and turn it over to the bookkeeping office. Then he'd lather up his hands to wash off the germs from the coins that had passed through his fingers, remove his white smock and cap, put on his jacket and fedora, and go slowly home for lunch.

✦ ✦ ✦

Hersh Levinzon was by nature satisfied with his lot, but then it's not hard to be happy when things go well. His children, thank God, had good jobs. He himself was in perfect health and earning his own bread. Above all, his beloved Ester was as beautiful as ever, still doing the housework as energetically as she had fifty years ago, still quiet and reserved—the exact opposite of Avrom's wife, Mira. Often Avrom said to Ester, loud enough for Mira to hear: "Mama, in this house you're in charge just as much as Mira. You're not dependent on anyone's charity, so don't worry about what she likes or doesn't like. Just do as you please." He took his wife aside and told her to watch her temper. "Show me a man who loves his mother," he said, "and I'll show you a man who loves his wife." Before she could reply, he closed her mouth with a kiss. And so the household was quiet and peaceful, despite Mira with her strong opinions. During the week they stayed out of one another's way and ate separately, but on Friday and Saturday evenings the family gathered in the big dining room for the Sabbath. "Queen Ester," in her embroidered white blouse and long diamond earrings, would say the blessings over the candles and quietly wish the family a "*gut shabbos.*" Then she'd straighten the lacy scarf on her head and take her seat in the place of honor to the left of her husband. Avrom sat on his father's right, with sullen Mira by his side.

Hersh Levinzon was not overly observant, just moderately so. He didn't bother the Almighty very often, and by the same token preferred that the rabbis and such would mind their own business when it came to his affairs. But he was strict about observing the Sabbath and the holidays and loved the special cleanliness of those days, the delicious smells and tasty dishes, every bite taken with the knowledge that he wasn't just eating but fulfilling the commandment to partake of the ritual foods. Avrom arranged with the pharmacy manager that the old man would always have Shabbos off, as well as the holidays, and both sides were satisfied. Avrom Grigorievitsh tended to get his way. With the help of a single pair of top-quality imported eyeglasses, Avrom Grigorievitsh could, if he so chose, find a solution to the most complicated problem, the kind that no one else could resolve. Whenever there was trouble, everyone came straight to him.

"Why can't you take care of this foolishness, Avreyml?" his father said irritably. "You've got the brains—make them back off. Not legally married all of a sudden—it's ridiculous! What do they want from me at my age?"

"They don't want anything, Dad, they just need a certificate from ZAGS saying that you're really married."

"What do you mean 'really'? How do they think we're married—for make-believe? Rabbi Vaysberg, a relation of Rabbi Tsirelson himself, officiated at the wedding, and now some *sheygets* comes along and asks if we're really married. I'm telling you, the world has turned upside down."

Avrom saw that it wasn't worth arguing. In his father's view, the chairman of the city council was a *sheygets* and the manager of ZAGS a snub-nosed *shiksa*. Even if you could have brought Rabbi Tsirelson and his relation Rabbi Vaysberg back from the dead, plus all the other town leaders from back then, it wouldn't have done any good. Avrom calmed his father down, told him he was getting upset over nothing, and promised to take care of everything. The next day he took the old couple down the street to ZAGS to sign the necessary papers.

Ester put on her Shabbos dress and her white crocheted shawl.

"What's the special occasion?" Hersh said. "Has some miracle occurred? Are we celebrating?"

"Stop, Hershl!" she said. "What are you so angry about? It's not your son's fault. I can't very well go out dressed like a pauper when my child—no Evil Eye—has such an important job."

"Your child, your child," he teased. "The guy runs an empire and to her he's still a child."

Ester smiled. She knew her husband was like a match— quick to flare up, quick to cool down. "Go change your jacket, Hershl," she said softly, and he did.

At the registry office, they were shown to two armchairs. Everything had been worked out in advance with Avrom Grigorievitsh. The "wedding contract" had been typed up, and only a few details were missing.

"Where, in what city, did the wedding take place?" the official asked.

Hersh Levinzon had decided that since the conversation was taking place in Russian they could manage without him. He was busy examining the office, with its fine drapes, its massive desk, and its large portrait of Brezhnev on the eastern wall, as befitted a living saint, and didn't hear the question. Avrom leaned toward his father and quietly repeated: "Father, do you remember where the wedding took place?

"What do you mean, do I remember? I'll tell you exactly where. I was called to the Torah in Căușeni, and . . ."

Avrom didn't hear the rest. His eyes filled with tears as he struggled not to laugh. The formalities were concluded, the papers signed. They took their leave and went out into the corridor.

"Dad," Avrom said, "what world are you living in? It's not the old days anymore. Who cares whether you were called to the Torah? You're not supposed to talk about things like that—and you were getting ready to tell them all about the *haftarah* too. Don't you realize—these days when you say someone's been called to the Torah, you mean he's been called up by the NKVD. And if he's reading from the *haftarah*, God forbid, he's in prison."

On the way back, no one said a word. At home Hersh took off his good jacket and threw it on the floor—most unlike him. He barely touched the lunch Ester prepared, even though none of it was her fault. She barely understood what was going on, with one laughing and the other sulking. Asking questions would only make things worse, she decided, so she kept quiet and tried to calm everybody down. She didn't learn the whole story until years later, when her husband was already in the next world and Avrom was recounting the so-called "episode" to guests gathered around the beautifully set dining room table. From her usual seat at the head of the table, beside the empty armchair, she gave Avrom a puzzled look. She still didn't understand.

"What's so funny?" she asked. "They did call your father, may he rest in peace, to the Torah in Căuşeni. I remember it like yesterday. The wedding itself was in Bender. The whole city made a fuss over us."

"Oh, Mom." Avrom gave her a tender hug. "May you live to a hundred and twenty."

✦ ✦ ✦

In the 1970s, when the great emigration occurred, Avrom
was among those who moved to Israel. By then his
mother was long gone and his wife Mira had died young
after a long, hard illness. He came with his son and his
son's family. Although by then he was close to seventy, he
had no trouble settling in and quickly found a part-time
job in a pharmacy. He was lonely, though. Accustomed
to being busy, he didn't know what to do with his free
time. So when his brother, who'd been in the country for
years, introduced him to Rokhl, a lovely widow with a
good pension, he wasted no time. Before long they were
engaged. She wanted a religious wedding, and he agreed.
Why not? He'd been brought up in a Jewish home, hadn't
he? He wouldn't have any trouble reciting the necessary
words in Hebrew.

Unexpectedly, however, a problem arose. His wife's
death certificate from Kishinev, duly signed and stamped
according to Soviet regulations, had no standing with
the local rabbinate and was rejected out of hand. Rokhl's
husband's death certificate was strictly kosher—he'd died
in Israel—but Mira's was no good. What next? The rabbinical court had an administrative office and a secretary.
You made an appointment, and then you had to bring two
witnesses who would attest that you weren't just making
things up, your wife was really dead. Avrom was annoyed.
He wasn't used to such obstacles. But this was a new
country, he told himself, with new rules, and it was Israel,
after all, so it wasn't a question of anti-Semitism. With his
usual self-confidence, he didn't ask anyone for advice as
he prepared to appear before the court, relying instead
on his own intuition. Finding witnesses was no problem.

Soreh Vaysman, a fine, respectable woman who had been a neighbor in Kishinev, promised to show up, and an old friend of Mira's who'd settled in Bat Yam also agreed to do him a favor.

On the appointed date, Avrom rose at dawn, impatient for the day to begin. He paced back and forth, trying to kill time, but the hands of the clock barely moved. He went out onto the terrace to watch the street sweepers, then back inside again, until finally it was seven o'clock, when he called Mrs. Vaysman to make sure she was on her way. The friend from Bat Yam was also on time. Avrom met her at the station, gave her a kiss, and apologized for her trouble.

"Don't be silly, Avrom," she said. "Friends are friends."

There was no need to coach them. They'd both been at Mira's funeral. The one thing he made clear was that if they were asked if they were relatives of the Levinzons, they should answer definitively: "*lo*," no.

"Don't worry, Avrom, we know what to do," they said. "We're not children. The law is the same everywhere."

Everything seemed in place, but Avrom couldn't sit still. In the big waiting room, he kept getting up from the bench, pacing, sitting down again. All his nervous habits were on display. He hitched up his pants, adjusted his hat, and stood too close to whoever he was talking to, forcing the other person to back up, upon which he would hitch up his pants and step even closer, as if to pin the person to the wall. These mannerisms had shown up only in old age; when he was younger there'd been no sign of them. Now his nerves were getting the best of him.

He kept hitching up his pants and fiddling with his hat until finally the door to the courtroom opened and he heard his name being called. Ever the gentleman, he motioned the ladies in first and followed them into the room. Three judges sat at a table along the eastern wall as if in the synagogue. They were reading over some documents that must have been his.

The chief judge looked up and said "*Shalom*," then asked: "What are these ladies doing here?"

"These are my witnesses," Avrom answered firmly. "They are natives of Kishinev who attended my wife's funeral, may she rest in peace."

At this, the other two judges raised their heads and peered over their glasses as if inspecting some exotic creature that had somehow blundered its way into their presence. Avrom couldn't understand why they looked so puzzled. He started to say more, but the chief judge stopped him. "I see you're not a young man," he said. "You should know by now that under Jewish law, it is improper for women to bear witness in a rabbinical court."

"But they were both at the funeral," Avrom persisted. "Who could be more proper?"

"My friend," said the judge, "Jewish law is not to be debated. It is to be obeyed."

Avrom broke out in a sweat. "I haven't been in the country very long," he said. "I hardly know anyone. Where am I supposed to find witnesses?

"Ask around," the judge replied. "You'll find them."

"So," he said in Russian to the two women as they left the courtroom, "I guess we're not in the Soviet Union anymore. We're not only in a new country, we're in a new world—a world we know nothing about."

He wiped the sweat from his brow, hitched up his pants, and turned up his palms as if to say, "What did I do wrong?" The women assured him it was nothing, these things happened.

A week later he came back with two old men from his brother's synagogue. During the course of the week, Avrom had changed. He seemed diminished, bruised. This time around he felt utterly detached from what was happening.

Suddenly, as if it were years ago, he heard the question: "Where were you married?"

"In Kishinev," he said.

"And where were you called to the Torah?"

"I wasn't—"

All at once, as clear as day, his father appeared before his eyes with a thin smile on his lips. Avrom could have sworn he even saw him wink. He shook himself and leaned against the table.

"Yes," he heard himself say, as if in a dream. "Yes, I was called to the Torah in Căuşeni."

"And where is this Căuşeni?"

"It was once a Jewish town in Bessarabia."

AT THE WESTERN WALL

The night after they bought the car, Frida didn't sleep a wink. Every half hour she got out of bed and ran to the window to see if it was still there. The children kept reminding her that they were in Israel, not the Soviet Union, so the car didn't need to be locked in a garage, and they were right, but Frida was not convinced. It doesn't hurt to be careful, she said to herself. God helps those who help themselves. A chain is only as strong as its weakest link. And so on. The children had saved up to buy the car, their first expensive purchase in the new land. It was a used car that doubtless had already changed hands more than once, but it looked good—good enough to attract buyers, anyway. Each time the car had been led to the wedding canopy, Frida imagined, it was first immersed in a ritual bath, suitably anointed, and decked out in sumptuous attire like the most dazzling of brides.

Engine problems and other flaws would make themselves known soon enough, but for now it promised all sorts of pleasures—the very fact of owning a car, for one, and then the prospect of family trips to beautiful and interesting places.

For the grandchildren, the car was a given. Everybody had one. Nearly all their friends had had cars for ages, while they'd looked on enviously. Now they finally had theirs, and if anyone dared to breathe a word against the Subaru . . .

The young couple kept things close to the chest. They smiled and took care of everything on their own without a word in front of Mother. Otherwise they knew she'd ruin everything by asking how much did this cost, and how much was that, and even crazier questions—had they had the car inspected, did it have all its documents, was there a lien against it? The things old people think of! In fact, though, they knew they'd been too trusting. The idea of a lien hadn't even entered their heads.

As a child, Frida had never ridden in a car. She hadn't even set foot outside her *shtetl* until she was twelve— after which, however, she'd been sent away to a big-city school and lived through the hunger and privation of the war. For her, every penny counted. It was hard to watch the children spending recklessly. But it wasn't her job to meddle or give advice, and she'd never dream of driving a wedge between husband and wife. So she closed her eyes to a lot of things, pretending not to see, and then at night she tossed and turned.

Today they were on their way to Jerusalem. She'd spent the past few days preparing food for the journey—light, simple things that would be easy to eat during the trip.

Everything was in the refrigerator, enough for the whole family for the whole day. Let the children laugh, but could they do any better? With her mix of small-town and big-city experience, she had something to teach those two. Every day, it seemed, something new came along that she'd never get the hang of, but she consoled herself with what she did keep up with—and even more with all that she knew about a vanished world. She was a living witness to a time and place that today even the most highly educated people could learn about only in books.

◆ ◆ ◆

In the days of horse and wagon, the question of who sat where was very important. A merchant setting off on a business trip would make sure to buy a prestigious forward-facing seat. It would not do to sit with his back to the horse, or people would stick their heads out the windows and cluck in sympathy—clearly he was slipping, maybe even going bankrupt. At the height of the season, drivers would fleece their customers by selling the place of honor twice, forcing two to squeeze into a single seat. The unlucky passengers could hardly sue the driver, who was struggling to support a family on next to nothing. Also, everyone knew that a driver was no rabbi, you couldn't expect to take him at his word. Besides, there was no other way to get around.

The seat next to the driver always went to someone who was either too poor or too young to care where he sat.

These days, like everything else, this system had been turned upside down. The head of household was at the wheel with his wife beside him, both in sunglasses and looking very pleased with themselves. The rest of the family sat happily in the back. Every seat felt like a place of honor.

Frida sat in the middle, a grandchild on either side. This arrangement was necessary to prevent fights. The kids were always arguing, and sometimes the arguments came to blows. Recently, believe it or not, a quarrel had broken out over Ahasuerus, the Persian king in the Book of Esther. The granddaughter, the older one, took the position that Ahasuerus was a big jerk. Her brother stuck up for the king on the grounds that he'd saved the Jews just in time.

"So what?" said the granddaughter. "What does that have to do with—"

It was all too complicated for a five-year-old to handle with words. He reached over and gave his sister a slap, unintentionally jabbing Grandma in the side as well.

This time, Frida had a plan. In preparation for their first visit to the Western Wall, she'd entertain them with a story. They loved her stories, didn't they? They'd behave themselves and learn something at the same time.

The strategy worked like a charm. There wasn't a peep out of them. They leaned against her, hanging on every word without a single interruption. Even the adults up front stopped their whispering and listened in. The story was new to them, it seemed, even though when they were younger they must surely have learned about the destruction of the Temple from Feuchtwanger's *The Jewish War*.

Frieda herself had forgotten much that she used to know, but she tried to convey what she did remember as clearly as possible. It was a pleasure to tell the story. She could feel herself growing bigger in her own eyes. You see, she said to herself, I'm still worth something after all. I do have something to teach.

The Wall made them quiet. They stopped talking and stepped softly, careful not to dishonor the holy site, all that remained of the Temple and the wall that had once surrounded it. The spirit of the place cast a powerful spell. Hearts pounding, they couldn't help reaching out to touch the ancient stones overgrown with moss. Frida looked at the women standing in prayer, some old, some young, some motionless in their ecstasy, others swaying fervently. A mixture of envy and awe stole over her. The women looked utterly in earnest. Could they possibly believe that stuffing notes into the crevices in the Wall would bring them any more attention than the screams and pleas that rose from the gas chambers at Auschwitz and Treblinka? Yet they were appealing to that same wrathful God, trusting that same Father in Heaven to attend to the slightest moan, the least lament voiced by His creatures. They must be another kind of Jew, Frida said to herself. A very different kind.

Frida's throat knotted up. She tightened her grip on her grandson's hand and stepped away from the Wall. But a woman in some kind of festive costume was blocking their way. A Yemenite with a tray of sweets in her hands. Please, would they take a cookie? Startled, Frida wrenched herself out of her thoughts. She glanced at the colorful treats in their pleated paper cups. They looked strange, not at all like the spiced honey cake and fruitcake she knew from back home. She thanked the woman politely, as she would have back in the *shtetl*, and indicated that she wanted to get by. But her grandson had reached up to take a cookie—two cookies. *"Mazel tov!"* he said to the woman in a loud, clear voice.

"A blessing on your little head, *hamud sheli.*" The Yemenite beamed down at the boy. "And on your grandmother, too. She should live to see your bar mitzvah and bring honor to the Wall, like me on this day."

Frida began to tremble with shame. She had committed a terrible sin, insulting a woman who'd approached her in friendship. Here in Israel, it seemed, a child was more in the know than an old woman. Her grandson had figured out right away that the woman was handing out sweets in honor of her child's *yom huledet,* his birthday, and had immediately offered the proper congratulations. Frieda had been witless, stupid. She stammered an apology, took a cookie from the tray, struggled to think of something to say.

"Don't worry, it's nothing," the woman said soothingly. "Someday we'll learn to get along and live together as one. The young people are better at it than we are."

On the way home, Frida felt so ashamed that she didn't open her mouth. She kept kissing the grandchildren, patting their hands. What a country this is, she couldn't stop thinking, where as a new chapter of life begins, the children are teaching their elders how to be Jewish.

THE CAP

The door gave a creak, and before Dina could get out of her chair, Ofer was standing in the doorway with his backpack.

"Darling, you're here!" Dina stood on tiptoe to give her grandson a hug and a kiss.

"Why do you leave your door open, *savta?*"

Dina looked at him, baffled. "What do you mean, open?" she said. "Can't you see the deadbolt?"

"Yes, *savta,* but it's not locked. You have to lock it."

Dina waved a hand and shrugged. "The important thing is that you're here," she said. "How long can you stay? Through Shabbos? Thank God. Does Mother know you're home? Yes or no?"

She talked and talked, not letting him get a word in. She wanted to know everything: was the blister on his heel still bothering him, had he brought his laundry home, and again, did his mother know he was here? It was a little surprising that he'd come to her before his parents, but after all she was no stranger—he'd grown up at her knee. She'd fussed over him since the day he came home from the hospital, had bathed him while tenderly singing her mother's lullaby: "Into the water baby goes, God bless baby's ten pink toes." Rina had stood nervously by her side. "Sing the song, Mama, sing it!" She had faith that the Yiddish blessing would work wonders.

Ofer leaned his rifle in the corner, took off his heavy pack, and removed his cap, which his grandmother had dubbed a *varenik* because it looked like a half-moon dumpling. He reached for the plate of cinnamon cookies without bothering to wash his hands.

"These are delicious, *savta*! Thumbs up!"

"Enjoy, darling," she said. "I made them just for you."

"I could smell them on the way here."

"Aha! So that's why you came to me instead of Mother."

"Stop, *savta*, you're insulting me!"

Dina shook her head—he knew her and her cutting remarks all too well. She felt a flicker of doubt. Why was he speaking Yiddish so fluently? Maybe all this was a dream—the clever kind of dream that feels absolutely real until it fizzles into nothing, and then you wake up feeling like a fool. But no, it couldn't be, not this time. The proof was that the cinnamon cookies smelled so good. You wouldn't smell cinnamon in a dream. Also the *varenik*, the cap. She'd seen him wearing it for the first time the other week, when they'd gone to Hulda for the induction ceremony. That had been no dream, of that she was a hundred percent sure. It was a day she would never forget, a day when she'd felt as never before—pathetic as it may sound—that finally they were part of the country, part of the people, part of everything happening in Israel. Her heart filled with joy. A voice inside tried to hold her back—in Israel one tries not to show one's feelings—but she didn't listen. First of all, no one could tell what she was feeling, and second, she didn't care. She'd suffered enough in her life, had sat through enough occasions at the end of the table like a charity case with a fake smile on her lips, pretending she didn't feel like an outsider—though in fact she probably hadn't fooled a soul. In her old age she had the right to throw herself wholeheartedly into the ceremony for her grandson, and if people didn't understand, that was their problem, not hers.

All along the way in the car she'd sat looking out the window, turning things over in her mind and reciting blessings over the green meadows, the tall trees, the fat cattle grazing in the fields.

"Mama, are you comfortable back there?"

"Yes, why?"

"You're so quiet. It's not like you."

"I'm praying."

The military grounds began filling up—at least one carload per soldier, as well as buses carrying three or four families at a time. An old woman was being taken off one of the buses in a wheelchair. Dina was surprised. In the old days, the best an old woman could hope for was a place beside the stove and a glass of tea with jam. That passed for a good old age, even an enviable one. Today, though, an old woman wasn't content with a spoonful of jam. Wheelchair or no, she went to her grandchild's swearing-in ceremony along with everyone else. It looked to Dina as if something was bothering the old woman, even though her children were gathered around, straightening her clothing and smoothing her hair. An old person could always find something to be dissatisfied about, Dina knew from experience. She would have liked to watch the scene to the end and perhaps even put a word in, but she couldn't, because just then more buses pulled up, the soldiers were led in, and the crowd began to cheer. Finding your own soldier in the group was impossible—they all looked alike, all of them covered with dust from head to toe and all topped with the same *varenikes*. But the soldiers, with their young eyes that could see for miles, came running into the arms of their families, who smothered them with kisses.

"You too, *savta*! You came all this way!"

"Of course I came. You're my grandson, aren't you? If that old *bubbe* in the wheelchair can make it, why not me on my own two legs? But Hershele"—she used his Yiddish name—"why are you all so dirty? Are you planning to take the oath like that?

"Don't worry, *savta*. The IDF will take care of everything"—and with that a signal sounded and he went running back to his group.

"Why do they have to treat the kids like this?" Dina said. "Even on a day like today they make them march through ten kilometers of mud."

"If it were up to you, Mama, they'd all be relaxing at a spa in honor of the occasion," her daughter said. "Maybe to us they're still children, but here they're soldiers."

Dina looked down and scuffed her toe in the dirt. She didn't like being criticized, even good-naturedly.

"Come, Mama, let's find our seats."

"You go ahead," Dina said. "I'll follow you."

I need a moment to sulk, she said to herself, but she quickened her pace to keep up with the children.

"One, two, three ... attention!" she kept hearing from all directions. The commanders, doubtless still children in their mothers' eyes, were ordering the soldiers to change into their dress uniforms and polish their boots for the ceremony.

Dina turned from side to side as the cries of "Attention!" rang out around her. As she compared this "*Hakshev!*" with the Russian "*Slushay!*" of her younger years, her eyes filled with tears. Who cares about the old days anymore, she thought to herself. No one has the patience, the time, or the desire to think about anything from before the State of Israel. Other things are always more important here. Back then we were remnants of the decadent bourgeoisie, and now we're remnants of exile. Dina didn't want to be a remnant anymore. She gave herself over to the public event, whispered the oath with the soldiers, sang the national anthem.

Had all this happened or not? Why did she suddenly have the feeling that Ofer's arrival today might be nothing more than a dream? She picked up his laundry, put the cap on top, and for some reason went to the door, which was still wide open. The cap fell off and started rolling down the stairs.

How annoying! Dina put down the clothes so she could chase after the cap. But she could barely move her feet, they were suddenly full of lead, and the cap ... as if possessed by a demon, it jumped down the steps, its visor spinning around and around as if to tease her. The little rascal is going to make me break my neck, Dina grumbled. But she kept going. The damn thing wasn't going to get the better of her. Besides, it was a military cap, not really a *varenik*, as she'd dubbed it in fun. What grief would befall Hershele if she didn't catch up with his cap? In Russia, a soldier who lost a cap could pay with his head. It was no small thing, a missing cap. First it could be interpreted as a form of insolence, and from there was just a short step to treason. Oy, the interpreting, the analyzing, the endless finger-pointing over supposed violations of the laws meant to protect the country from its innumerable enemies. The only force that united the vast country from end to end was fear. Fear worked itself deep into one's bones and was difficult to let go of even after one had escaped. At this moment, Dina was fully aware that she was no longer in Russia and that even the oldest commander in the army was a Jew, with a Jewish mother and maybe even a Jewish grandmother at home, which meant that everything was all right, wasn't it? Even so, she worried. What did they do to a soldier who lost a cap here in Israel? Meanwhile, the cap kept on rolling—down the stairs, through the door, and into the mud.

How had so much mud gotten into the courtyard? And since when was the courtyard enclosed on all sides, like back home? Not only that—the mud wasn't sandy and crumbly like the mud here. It was wet, like clay or sour cream. And there lay the cap with its visor in the air.

Not good, Dina thought. In the army for all of two weeks and already breaking rules. If she'd been alone, with no one watching, she would have rolled up her sleeves and marched right over to pick up the cap. But now the courtyard had filled up with soldiers, just like the other week at the training grounds, and all of them were smiling and looking at the cap.

"One, two, three, attention!" Dina heard the command loud and clear. "No laughing at the old woman! She's Hershele's grandma and she's baked us some delicious cinnamon cookies."

Dina was taken aback. It wasn't out of the question that the commander would know who she was. But delivering his orders in Yiddish? She must be dreaming, she thought—dreaming in Yiddish. And why not? People dreamed in Spanish, in Turkish, in Greek—why not in Yiddish?

The soldiers obeyed orders, hiding their smiles under their wispy mustaches. Then the very smallest of them all emerged from the group, picked up the cap, and held it out to her.

Dina screwed up her courage. "Please, children," she said, "could you ask your commander what happens under Israeli law when a soldier loses a cap? I'd like to know."

"Right away, *savta!*"

Br-r-r-ing! Just then the telephone rang and Dina opened her eyes.

Typical, she thought. Whenever she had a question, something always got in the way and she never received an answer. No one ever had a moment to spare. For a moment her eyes rested on the plate of cookies on the table. Then she smiled to herself and went to answer the phone.

INGATHERING OF EXILES

I don't know about other cities, but in Haifa the street called Kibbutz Galuyot—Ingathering of Exiles—is truly worthy of the name. Other cities may have bestowed the name when the street was still under construction, without knowing whether it would turn out to be a good fit. In Haifa, though, the street was already in its glory when it got its name. If they'd called it Kibbutz Olamot—Ingathering for Eternity—that wouldn't have been wrong either. The street must date back to the Ten Commandments, maybe even back to the Creation. Certainly it's as chaotic as the dawn of time—a bedlam of languages from all corners of the earth. People quarrel in Hebrew to get a point across; to show how important they are they fling insults in Russian; and to pull out all the stops they curse in Yiddish. Sometimes a few punches are even thrown, but by now the scrappiest old fighters have passed on, and these days people don't want to get their hands dirty. When a skirmish breaks out, most of the time the police don't even hear about it; the parties patch it up among themselves.

Residents of Haifa don't particularly boast about the street, but they're not ashamed of it either. It's like a part of the body you don't want to show off but can't do without. People who live in affluent neighborhoods like Denia and Ahuza are always coming down to Kibbutz Galuyot to get an old tool soldered or a musical instrument repaired, or to hunt for a bargain on an old-fashioned flatiron, a copper mortar, a samovar. Who needs such things, you ask? Good question. The answer: restoring antiques and decorating your parlor with them is the latest fad, and you can't find such things at the big Carmel market for any amount of money. So people hop into their shiny new cars and drive down to Kibbutz Galuyot to see what they can find.

Haifa residents do, anyway. Tourists content themselves with looking down from the terraces, which is too bad, because you can't see much from above—only a tangle of streets, lanes, back alleys. The best way to explore Kibbutz Galuyot is up close, provided it's not Shabbat. On Shabbat, the day of rest, all you can see is doors, mostly iron ones, bolted and locked with a thousand locks, as if to protect untold fortunes. There's not a soul on the street, except maybe a black cat, omen of bad luck, that has forgotten about the holy day and is out looking for someone's path to cross.

On Sunday, though, no matter how early you arrive, the place will be swarming with cars and people. For all I know, the congestion may even begin Saturday evening, the minute the Sabbath is over. But I'm getting ahead of myself. I was about to say there are almost no signposts on Kibbutz Galuyot. One or two handwritten ones, perhaps, but only to attract attention, not to point the way. People already know where to go, and besides, everything is in full view, either spread out on the sidewalks or hanging in the doorways.

Take the first store on the right, for example. The owner, Nakhman Zeyde, is quite the character. He sells only what fits in front of his door. Why? Very simple. He won't go anywhere near the mountain of wares he could choose from down the block, not for all the money in the world, because he knows that if he tried to display one more thing there would be no room for his chair, which is right where he likes it, next to the door, sheltered from sun and rain. No matter when you come, he'll be sitting there reading his newspaper, *Viața noastră*, which tells you he's a Romanian Jew. He's not old, Nakhman Zeyde, but not young either. In winter he wears a knit cap pulled down to the top of his glasses and a long coat that extends to his ankles. Judging by the fabric and style—ten buttons as big as plates, five to a row—it was made for him when he got married. I once bought a cast-iron pot from Nakhman Zeyde, and he was very pleased, not so much with the sale itself as with our friendly conversation, our mutual appreciation of old things. He hates it, he says, when people come asking "What's this, what's that?" These types, he says, aren't customers, they just get on his nerves and distract him from his paper. Nakhman Zeyde is not desperate for business. His pitchers and ladles and saucepans and Primus stoves will sell one of these days, and meanwhile they don't cost him anything. He has a good meal waiting at home regardless, says he. So you have to wonder why he drags himself to the store every day, rain or shine. And when I say drag, I mean drag. He can't stand up without splaying his feet sideways, and since he suffers from asthma, he pants and gasps on the way to his door, pants as he unlocks it, and gasps some more as he bends down to reach the bottom locks. He claims to be wealthy and says he comes to the shop only for the exercise and to get out and see people. I have my doubts, but who's to say?

Across the street, Moyshe Grynman describes himself the same way: he's rich and doesn't need the money. Him I believe, even if he is Polish. You can tell he's got money by the signet ring on his finger. He looks about seventy-five, and all things considered he seems to be doing well. Ramrod straight and always dressed to the nines in a sharp suit and tie. He sells ready-to-wear clothing, second-hand of course, mostly men's—he's not interested in women's clothes unless you hand them over for free, and even then he's picky. He doesn't pay much for men's clothes either, always acting as if he's doing you a favor as he examines each item and points out the imperfections—a stain here, a patch there. Even if the garment is in perfect condition, he'll find something wrong with it: no one wears such old-fashioned pants anymore, he'll grumble, they never sell. So he says, all the while not letting the pants out of his hands. Then he slips you a little something and you leave with no pants and barely enough money for the bus fare home. Quite the businessman. Though I must admit he has hands of gold. He can take old, wrinkled clothes, press and clean them, hang them up, and they'll look brand new, just like in a fancy store.

I've had occasion to study him closely, this Moyshe Grynman, because the window in front of my desk at work faces his store. A window is no small thing, especially one that overlooks Kibbutz Galuyot. It's a welcome bonus on top of my modest salary—but I keep that to myself. There's no reason my bosses need to know. I have not one but three bosses, all fellow countrymen from back home, and the tales I could tell ... but let's not get into that. Business is business, my bosses like to say, and they take the idea to extremes. If a poor man comes in begging for charity, they'll put him through the wringer, demanding to know how much he really has in the bank, and only after that will they go over to the drawer and pull out some magnificent sum—say, twenty agorot—and since in the old currency that was 2,000 lirot, they act as if they're being extremely generous.

But let's move on. We pass a few shops and come to Shloyme Stolyer, who used to be a carpenter and claims, like the others, that he keeps his hand in not for the money but only out of habit and to maintain his health. I have no idea what he's actually worth, but they say he's loaded. I call him Shloyme the Millionaire, even though the role of rich man suits him like a yarmulke on a pig. When it's hot he goes around shirtless, with his belly button hanging out like the young people, trying to blend in with the crowd. He looks ridiculous. When he comes in to see my bosses, even before saying good morning he'll mutter something confidential under his breath—"and seven," for example—meaning that the dollar is currently valued at 1.77 shekels. Every summer he goes on vacation in the Swiss Alps, and when he gets back he can't stop talking about what a surprise it was to bump into his neighbor, a simple bookkeeper. It's not really surprising—the two of them are not all that different. Shloyme's missus, on the other hand, is something special. Every day, this belle of Kibbutz Galuyot shows up slathered with make-up and dressed in the latest fashion. She stands around in her white pants, showing off her figure. Now and then she straightens old nails with a hammer or holds a board for him while he works a saw. The real reason she's there is to keep an eye on her husband and make sure he doesn't slip any money to his two married daughters from his first wife. Everything has to go to their son, she insists. The rich man suffers, but what can he do? Everyone has troubles; this is his.

Not far from Shloyme's, we come to the only butcher shop in the neighborhood. The only things left from the original store are a chopping block and hooks for hanging meat. The rest of the place is totally up to date, with all the necessities—tiled walls, a washstand for ritual ablution, an electric saw for bones and frozen meat, and on the desk a Japanese calculator, ledger, and checkbook. Needless to say, there's a kosher supervisor, an unusual one, very young and not bad-looking, you could even say handsome, but far too impressed with his own appearance. You can see him making his way down the street, posing next to cars and gazing into side mirrors as he twirls the long curls at his temples, humming happily to himself. He spends as little time in the butcher shop as possible—only as long as it takes to pick up the package that's waiting for him—then makes his way down the street, not just singing but practically dancing, with the parcel wrapped in a newspaper under his arm. He reminds me of the Jews back in Russia who used to bundle up their prayer shawls in newspaper, so as not to attract attention, when they walked to the synagogue on the Sabbath.

There are other stores just like the ones I've described, as well as two banks and an office of the rabbinate, but the real leaders of the street, the big shots, are the owners of the warehouses filled with "old things," in this case old furniture. I'm not talking about the Arabs who go from house to house collecting old clothes. This is different. When you want to get rid of an old piece of furniture, you call one of these warehouses and arrange for them to come out and take a look. When they arrive, no matter what amount you've jotted down, they offer you a tenth, and you accept whatever they say. You're at their mercy because you need room for your new furniture. In the warehouses the old furniture is repaired, restored, sanded, and varnished until it looks like new. The owners are true professionals, mostly young guys who started out as errand boys, worked their way up, and eventually inherited the business, including the store, the inventory, the reputation, even the few words of Yiddish they learned on the job. Unlike the old shopkeepers on the street, the young ones are in it for the money, not for fun, and they mean business. They're also gifted at keeping the peace. In the narrow street, if one car hits another and dents a fender or knocks out a headlight, someone will appear out of nowhere and take charge. A whisper into an ear here, a murmur there, a flurry of banknotes, a handshake, problem solved. As I said, the people on the street want nothing to do with police, write-ups, fines.

And now we come to the jewel in the crown—*Shuk HaPishpeshim*, the flea market. Fleas: ever since these disgusting vermin appeared on the face of the earth, we

Jews have bestowed their name on a host of markets, including Haifa's. The sign on the arch doesn't actually mention fleas—it says *Shuk Hrukhlim*, the vendors' market—but it means the same thing. To get in, you take a few steps down into a giant courtyard. I went once, just out of curiosity, and I couldn't believe my eyes. Endless rows of stalls—a hundred? a thousand?—with narrow aisles in between for customers. Every stall had a roof; otherwise the heat would have been unbearable. From a distance the place looked like barracks in a prison camp, but piled with old clothes instead of people. These are the piles that shopkeepers like Moyshe Grynman won't go near. Within them, I swear, lies a century's worth of clothing fashions. If you know what to look for, you can find antique garments here that belong in a museum: clothes for the Sabbath and clothes for everyday, wedding gowns and funeral attire, uniforms and costumes, overcoats and dressing gowns, fur coats and crinolines, fedoras and top hats. Impossible to list them all. Clothes that have gone in and out of fashion a thousand times. A girl might come upon an old-fashioned pelisse, a cape, and call it a poncho. Fine, it's a poncho, so long as she buys. Customers aren't easy to come by here, so when they show up the vendors don't let them out of their hands until they make a deal. They lose a little money here, make some there—it all works out in the end.

When an elderly couple dies, what happens to their belongings? This is a sight to behold. As soon as the second member of the couple closes his or her eyes, immediately after the *shivah*, the heirs waste no time. The ground burns under their feet, there's no time for sorting, everything must go. The vendors often get it all for no more than the cost of gas, driver, and wages for those who haul the junk away. The idea is to clear out the flat as quickly as possible. Once the truck is loaded, it goes straight to Kibbutz Galuyot, the cemetery of old things, and when people see the truck coming, they come running and fall on it like worms on a corpse. This one grabs a shirt, that one a pair of pants, this one a robe, that one a tablecloth, cups, teakettles, a kosher cutting board, a noodle pot, a wall clock, a pair of new shoes. Everything goes. Amid the pushing and shoving, the driver can barely manage to stuff the cash into his pockets fast enough. Trampled underfoot on the dirty sidewalk are towels, bedsheets, and blankets that housewives have spent years caring for, washing and ironing, mending and folding. Even before the soul has risen to stand before the Heavenly Throne, not a trace of the departed remains here on earth.

So when old residents of Haifa raise their eyes to the sky and piously intone that this is the street where the city got its start, I humbly submit that Kibbutz Galuyot is a place not only of beginnings but also of endings.

RETIREES

Lekh lekha le-artsekha . . .
Go forth to your land, and there you will see how great a
nation you are.

Every distinguished retiree in Elisheva Garden, our city
park, has a bench of his own. Not a whole bench to himself, of course—other people sit there with him—but on
his designated bench he's the central figure, the most out-
spoken, the expert, the analyst, and the chief commenta-
tor. No matter the topic at hand, old or new, political or
economic, he's ready with an opinion. For this reason, the
bench is known by his name, as if it were his private club.

He may not be the tallest or biggest on the bench, but
you can spot him a mile away by his confident stride, the
pipe he rarely smokes but never takes out of his mouth,

and the newspaper sticking out of his pocket. By these signs you know he's the leader, the spokesman.

Sharing Benderski's bench with him are three fellow retirees. Each of the four has a specific role to play, like the four children in the Passover Haggadah.

The leader is never the first to arrive. His followers are always waiting for him, and when they see him coming they move over to free up the seat of honor. Alter Serebrinski, who's known as Sir Walter, the deputy leader and chief wisecracker of the group, purses his lips and lets loose with his famous whistle, never failing to add, "Please move over so Khana Moyshe-Yoynes can sit down." No matter how many times he's asked about this Khana Moyshe-Yoynes, all he'll say is that his late mother used to pronounce these words every evening when she finished the housework and came out onto the porch. His mother, he assures them, wasn't one to say such a thing for no reason. At one time there must have been a rich woman in town who made people give up their seats.

A stranger will never sit on the bench, not because the seats are reserved, but because the leader will give him a look, silently asking who he is and what he's doing there. You don't simply choose a bench and sit down—you find a place where you're welcome, where you can comfortably speak your mind.

Young people are seldom seen in the park. They have other places to go, and when they do show up, they don't need benches. They can sit down on the grass without being afraid they won't be able to get back up again. They spread out blankets in the shade, lay out cups and plates, and enjoy a meal with their children in the bosom of nature. The older people come for other reasons: to get out of the house, to catch a breath of fresh air, and especially to add the latest news to their constant diet of newspapers, radio, and television. Any scrap of information is welcome, new or old. They don't mind hearing a story more than once, so long as it's told well.

Most people on the benches like to have their say. Often one interrupts another and there's a bit of a scene, until the "chairman" takes the pipe out of his mouth and calms everyone down. There are also people of few words who listen patiently and give everyone a chance to speak even if they don't agree. Fine, whatever you say, anything to keep the peace. After all, it's not as if the fate of the country will be decided on this bench. Naturally, such people are few and far between. To tell the truth, there may be only one in the whole bunch. Most would rather argue—and why not? Life is short—why not express yourself? There will be plenty of opportunity to remain quiet in the grave.

When the sun sinks down behind the last row of trees and there, in her modesty, throws off her lace-trimmed robe of fire and sinks into the cool sea to purify herself after her daily climb through the sweltering heavens, then Avrom Benderski removes his old Swiss watch from his pocket, presses the button to open the gilded cover, puts the piece to his ear to make sure it's running, and brings the meeting to a close. "Gentlemen," he says, "it's time to go home for supper."

1. THE WISE CHILD: CHAIRMAN AVROM BENDERSKI

The group that had stayed together like a family during the whole journey, from the railway station in Kishinev, to Kiev, to the famed station in Chop where they crossed over from Ukraine into Czechoslovakia, to the transit camp at Schönau Castle in Austria, where they waited for the flight to Israel—this band, united as they were by the travails of migration, fell apart as soon as the El Al plane from Vienna landed at the airport in Lod. As they made their way down the steps of the aircraft, they were still supporting and encouraging one another. But the minute they felt the ground under their feet and entered the reception hall, it was every man for himself, without a thought for his fellows. Having collected their bags and swallowed the traditional orangeade and sandwiches, they all rushed to telephone their relatives, who'd been made to wait in another room, as pandemonium would have ensued if they'd been allowed to meet the new arrivals on the second floor.

Avrom Benderski was well prepared for the reception procedure awaiting him at the long table in the next room. He knew exactly what to say and what housing to request. His older sister, who'd been in the country for years, had described everything in great detail in her letters. He could have sat down calmly and waited to be called, but he was too excited. Pacing back and forth, he noticed people lining up to use the telephone, so without thinking he got in line. Why not? He'd stood in enough queues back home, he could stand in a few more here. It was his first phone call in the new country. All he had to do was pick up the receiver and say the name, without even a number, and a minute later he heard Taybele's voice from the other room, in pure Yiddish: "Avreyml, is it you?" Tears flowed—it was a miracle!

All this was twenty years ago, in October of 1972. If he could have, he'd have planted a kiss on his own cheek to reward himself for the stubborn persistence with which he'd managed to overcome every obstacle placed in his path. Not only had he had to deal with officials, coworkers, and acquaintances who didn't want him to leave the Soviet Union, but getting his own family on board had also proved enormously difficult. Fortunately his son Igor was on his side, but his wife, daughter, and son-in-law were reluctant to give up their good jobs and their apartments full of modern appliances. They didn't want to see their wealth turn to dust, didn't want to pack their bags and go off to seek their fortune in a land where they didn't know a soul.

"We're not going to seek our fortune, you can get that out of your head," Avrom said angrily. "Our 'fortune' is that finally we have a land of our own. Finally we're allowed out of this hell where we're treated like garbage. Anti-Semitism is getting worse every day. Who knows how bad it's going to get? The hypocrites—on the one hand they can't stand us, they won't let our children into the university or give them jobs, and on the other hand they rant and rave that we're traitors, and how can we leave the fatherland where we're doing so well? As the Russians say, *'byot i plakat' ne dayot'*—they beat you and won't let you cry. Well, I've had it. My children don't know how to read or write a word of Yiddish. Can you blame me?—I've had enough. At least let my grandchildren grow up as proud Jews. Let them not be ashamed of their roots. Let them uphold the traditions. As for the things you can't bear to part with—all the more reason to get out. We've seen what can happen to a person's worldly goods. My father, Mendl Benderski, may he rest in peace, was known and respected all over town and owned a house with three big windows on Minkovsky Street. And what happened? Not just the house but Minkovsky Street itself was wiped off the face of the earth. Today all you see is a row of ten-story buildings flashing their windows at the stars as if they've been there forever. You could go crazy running around in that labyrinth trying to find the place where you grew up."

"Are you starting up again with the three windows on Minkovsky?" his wife asked. "You're making my head hurt."

"As long as you live, Sheyndele," said Avrom, "you'll never understand me. It's beyond you. You grew up in a communal apartment in Odessa where whole families were crammed in on top of one another, each with a little corner of the shared kitchen, and always a line for the toilet."

Fate played a trick on Avrom Benderski. After all those years of reproaching his Sheyndele for her obdurately Odessan approach to life, this same Yevgenia Piotrovna (whose name, of course, was not Yevgenia, nor was her father's name Piotr) caught on to the Israeli ways more quickly than anyone else. Stout and slow-moving as she was, she adapted with agility to the local customs, immediately learned the language, figured out the Israeli mentality, and assumed an air of supreme capability and reliability. Right away she was offered a job at the Sochnut, the immigrant absorption agency, and the Benderskis were moved to the head of the line for a coveted apartment. The forms with all the minutiae that baffled most new arrivals—What was the right answer to this question?

Why did they have to sign with only their initials instead of their whole name as they had since childhood?—all this Sheyndele handled effortlessly, as if she'd spent her whole life swimming in an ocean of red tape. Much to his embarrassment, Avrom Benderski, the head of household and chief breadwinner, was called in to sign on the dotted line only after everything was settled. Yaffa, as she was now known, Madam Benderski, was the leading lady. Nor did the situation change over the years. To this day, it was best to stay out of her way. She received her own pension, wore three jewel-trimmed gold necklaces, chaired the local branch of Na'amat, was an adviser to WIZO, and played an important role in public affairs throughout the country. She managed the home front as well. A cleaning woman came once a week. When Sheyndele had a free day, she might cook a tasty broth or a borsht, enough for the week. Otherwise she ordered in dishes from a neighborhood woman, and he, Avrom, ate the food and gave thanks, because what choice did he have? He wasn't about to chop her head off, or even divorce her, and he couldn't throw her out of the house because she was never home. Sometimes on a Friday when she was working in the kitchen, he'd plead with her. "Sheyndele," he'd say, "won't you bake me some of those pletzl rolls for Shabbos—the ones with sugar and cinnamon, or the poppy-seed kind? I'd love one of those rolls." She'd turn around with that double chin of hers, give him a look, and shrug her shoulders. "Nobody bakes those in Israel," she'd say, and she'd bring home a cheese pastry with raisins from the bakery.

Since he'd retired, his routine was to take a walk every morning and every evening, except on Sundays. On Sundays he volunteered as a counselor to the elderly at the social welfare office. He listened to people and told them where they could get their problems solved, and if they couldn't do it on their own he went with them. People were always waiting to see him, especially recent immigrants, because he knew so many languages. Sundays always put him in a good mood. The rest of the days were sometimes good, sometimes not.

◆ ◆ ◆

Late one Wednesday afternoon, who should show up near Elisheva Garden but "Sir Walter," Alter Serebrinski. He was deep in conversation with two people Avrom didn't recognize, both tall, one with a potbelly and the other thin as a reed. Alter was almost invisible between them. Avrom stopped and waited. Suddenly Alter looked up. "My God!" he exclaimed. "Avrom Benderski!" He shook his head to clear away the cobwebs, closed his left eye, which was not what it used to be, and peered through the right as if through a telescope.

"As I live and breathe," he said finally, "it's Avrom Benderski with the three windows on Minkovsky Street!"

"Sir Walter," Avrom said, "may you live and be well, with your tongue like a knife that you inspect every morning for a nick, a dent, or a blemish."

After such a meeting, I ask you, how could Avrom complain about family difficulties, immigration problems, or anything else? He wouldn't have been more delighted if he'd laid eyes on his own father, Mendl Benderski, the rich man with the house on Minkovsky Street, even though back in Kishinev he and Alter had not been on the best of terms. Back then, he, Avrom Benderski, a native of

the city, had had to answer to Alter Serebrinski, the pip-
squeak, who was only a meter and a half tall, whose feet
barely reached the floor when he sat in a chair, and who
was a newcomer to Kishinev, having arrived only after the
war with other refugees from towns that were no more.
But Alter was brilliant. If he hadn't been Jewish he would
have had a career in academia or at least in the finance
ministry. But since he was both Jewish and short, he rose
only to the rank of assistant to the chief bookkeeper for
"MoldauFrTorgTekstil"—a word that is very difficult to
translate into Yiddish or any other language. I don't think
there have ever existed such unintelligible tongue-twist-
ers as were abundant in the land of the Soviets. Twice a
year, Benderski had to appear before this institution and
deliver a report on the work at "LenRaiTorgTekstil," his
workplace, which occupied a lower rung in the hierarchy.

On one such occasion, he delivered his report as usual
not to the chief bookkeeper, who was only a figurehead
with a party card, but to Alter, his deputy, who was as
stubborn as he was short, and who would hit the ceiling
over the slightest deviation from the rules. This time,
when the deputy seized on a trivial detail that could easily
have been corrected on the spot, shoved the documents
across the table, and told him to come back when everything was in order, Benderski made up his mind and took
advantage of their being alone in the room to speak up.

"Serebrinski, my friend," he said calmly, "I've been
meaning to ask you something. What's a short guy like
you doing with such a long name? You're like a little kid
with a big fur cap. Do yourself a favor and change it. The
shorter the better. I'd suggest something like 'Sir Walter.'
What do you say?"

For a moment, Alter Serebrinski didn't know whether to laugh or to grab the insolent joker by the neck and throw him out of the room. He took off his glasses and gave Avrom a long look. Suddenly he felt a tickle in one nostril, which he understood as a warning. "Be careful, Alter," he said to himself. With a smile, he put his glasses back on and held out a hand. "Let me see your report," he said, switching into Yiddish. "The hell with the higher-ups. It won't kill them if everything isn't exactly the way it should be. Myself, I don't give a damn." He signed the papers. "Anyone who can come up with such a brilliant name," he said, "even if he does happen to be a native of Kishinev and an arrogant bastard—that man is a brother to me."

All these years later, God brought them together again in Ashdod. They went to the park and sat down on a bench under a tree, and that very day the cornerstone of "Benderski's bench" was laid. Why Benderski's, you ask? First, because of the two of them, Benderski was the genuine native of Kishinev. This is something Israelis can't understand. For them, the only pedigree that matters is the *sabra*'s—the one who was born here and whose roots in the country go back three, four, five generations. Everyone else belongs in the same category: diaspora Jews. But ask anyone from Kishinev and you'll find out immediately who's a native of the city and who isn't. That's number one. Number two, Avrom Benderski was the only one in the group who was a true pensioner. The rest may have called themselves pensioners, but they didn't actually receive pensions. They were on government assistance.

2. THE WICKED CHILD: SIR WALTER

Just as Avrom Benderski was not really the "wise child" of the group, so Alter Serebrinski was not really wicked. But the role of the wise child was already taken, and to call Alter simple would have been ridiculous. He agreed to take on the role of the wicked child after careful analysis. What, he asked himself, do we Jews mean when we call a person wicked? Do we mean to say he's a criminal? A lawbreaker? No. We need not look far for an example. Consider the "wicked" son in the Passover Haggadah—what did he do that was so terrible? All he did was to ask, "What does this Passover service mean to you?" "To you," rather than "to us." That was his sin in its entirety. For that we call him wicked? For that we affix such a label and pass it down through the generations? If you want my opinion, Alter told the group, a "wicked" child like that is superior to all the rest of the "children," wise and simple alike. Present company excluded, of course. We've all experienced our own "exodus"—from Russia, that is—but in my view, those who are known in the Haggadah as clever are simply those who understand how to phrase a question in such a way as to appear both quick-witted and pious. The "simple" ones, for their part, pretend to be naïve, but they're not really simple at all. Try stepping on the toes of one of these poor fools and watch him scream bloody murder, haul you before a rabbinical court, and sue the pants off you. That's why when it comes to the four children in the Haggadah, I consider the "wicked" one to be the most honest. He doesn't beat around the bush, he says what he thinks and demands that you tell him the truth in return, and then he'll decide how to proceed.

The group on the bench looks at him without understanding a word. Avrom Benderski is the only one who can follow his exploration of the fine points of Jewish law. It so happens that Avrom, too, was sent to a Talmud Torah and a Jewish secondary school—his father was determined to keep his offspring from turning their backs on Jewish culture—and so, many years later, when he arrived in Israel in his old age, he had no trouble with the language. Even so, he feels secretly envious of Alter—why, he's not sure, perhaps because he's so articulate. Not that Avrom himself is exactly tongue-tied; he never has to search for a word—but even so he knows he'll never be quite as smooth, as quick-witted, as fluent as his friend. Whenever Alter opens his mouth he sounds as if he's reading from a written document. It's not as bad as it could be, because Alter is not a show-off; he can be gracious and respectful … yet Avrom often feels outclassed. The one time Benderski tried to get the better of Serebrinski, back in Kishinev, he was almost sure he'd succeed, but in fact nothing came of it. This was the time when he came up with the name "Sir Walter" as a joke. Anyone else would have taken offense, flown into a rage, and thrown Avrom out of the office on his ear. Not Alter. He figured out how to finesse the situation perfectly, and in no time at all he had the upper hand and was looking down on Avrom from above, even though when he stood up straight he was no taller than a sitting dog. The name Sir Walter stuck, but not because of Benderski. Alter himself made it happen, because such a brilliant witticism, he said, was worth more than his own prestige. "Either you're born with it or you're not," he said

of Benderski's cleverness—"such a gift cannot be taught."
That night at home, when he told the story to his wife
Adel, he laughed and laughed. She looked at him as if he'd
lost his mind.

"What's the big joke?" she said. "He made fun of you."

"I know . . . but the way he did it!"

She would never understand. She was a native of
Kishinev.

This may be the place to make clear that Alter
Serebrinski held what you might call dual citizenship.
When necessary, he could claim to be from Kishinev. He
lived in Kishinev, his wife's family was from Kishinev, and
his two children had been born in Kishinev. Furthermore,
he knew the city backwards and forwards—its streets,
alleys and back alleys, and jokes and anecdotes going
back to when the city was nothing more than a southern
border town in the Russian Empire, in the days when Tsar
Alexander II had sent Pushkin, the god of Russian poetry,
into exile there to punish him for his treasonous political
views. He'd studied the upheavals that led to the pogroms,
the massacres of the Jews, and he knew all about how
Kishinev had become the capital of Moldova. Everything
interested him, he liked delving into things, both history
and current events alike. But when he wanted to, he could
go the other way, transforming himself into a man from
Alexăndreni, with all the gestures and expressions of a typical small-town resident. Unlike some, he wasn't ashamed
of his background and didn't try to hide it. In fact, he said,
if there was anything about him that was particularly
good or special, it was all thanks to his hometown. And
Alexăndreni, let me tell you, was about as small as a town
could be. It had only one street, and even that wasn't fully

finished, with a half-built house at the end. Hitler, may his name be erased, had destroyed the whole place.

Alter still remembers the good times, when the town was thriving and a man like his father could send his youngest son to Soroca to study at the Tarbut School. Why Soroca, when Bălți was closer? Because a wealthy relation in Soroca had taken an interest in the boy, who seemed to be turning out to be a prodigy. Maybe he saw in him a future son-in-law. He agreed to take him in as a boarder for a small sum. So Alter was exposed to all the ins and outs of Jewish life, and after graduating from secondary school he went on to the university in Bucharest.

Alter doesn't like to dwell on those years in Bucharest. Like the other Jewish students, he was beaten, especially during the time of the Goga-Cuza government, when anti-Semites were in power in Romania. He suffered terribly from hunger, and also from disappointment on the romantic front, which he blamed on his short stature, though inside he knew that wasn't the only reason. It was a wound he didn't like to probe too deeply. After his failed love affair, it took him a long time to get back on his feet. Years passed before he met Adel and married her.

His return home in 1940 is especially hard for him to talk about. He was then twenty-four years old. With his university diploma, he'd been drafted into the Romanian army for only one year instead of three. But in 1940, under the terms of the pact between Russia and Germany, our region of Bessarabia was taken away from Romania and incorporated into the Soviet Union. The Russians called it a "liberation," while the Romanians gnashed their teeth and called it an "occupation." The Jews danced in the streets with joy when the Romanian army withdrew, but the Romanians vowed they'd soon be back to settle accounts. Among the provisions of the pact was an agreement to free the Bessarabian soldiers who were then serving in Romania. These soldiers, including Corporal Alter Serebrinski, were indeed released. Famished and exhausted from walking (they were given no money for a train), they arrived at the Prut River and waited to cross the bridge to Ungheni, thus leaving Romania and entering the territory now under Russian control.

That's where it happened. The thugs in the Romanian border patrol took out all their rage on the poor Bessarabian soldiers, ordering them to take off their uniforms, including their boots, their socks, and even their undershirts, then turn over the bundle to the duty officer, after which they received a form and stood in line to cross the bridge clad only in their drawers. Alter, whose army clothes had never been the right size, stood frozen in place despite the summer heat. His underpants were not only too big but full of holes, and he didn't know what to do. No matter how he tried tying and adjusting them to conceal his private parts, a new hole would appear. He was beside himself.

"Hey, Bercu"—for Romanians, all Jews were either Bercu or Herşcu—"hold on to your junk, or all the girls on the other side are going to faint when they see it."

Alter stepped onto the bridge, his ears ringing with the jokes and laughter of the rowdy guards. So it has been for Jews since time began, he thought to himself—generation after generation standing in line naked, waiting to be beaten and whipped.

On the other side of the bridge, in Ungheni, a big crowd of relatives, friends, and curious onlookers had gathered to greet the newly liberated soldiers. Alter arrived bent over so far that his father had trouble finding him.

He buried his head in his father's chest and sobbed like a child. "Father," he cried, "I'll never forget this and I'll never forgive." Through his tears he noticed a girl with two long braids pointing him out to her mother and laughing.

More than half a century has passed since that day, yet even now he's tormented by the same recurring nightmare: He's standing on the other side of the Prut, by the bridge leading to Ungheni, and everyone is laughing at him. God in Heaven, he thinks to himself, I've been in Israel so long by now, why am I still afraid of them? And his Adel, who in the dream is the little girl with two long braids, is wagging her finger at him. "I told you not to get mixed up with those bandits!" she's saying. "How could you forget? Some people just go looking for trouble." Alter wakes up with no idea where he is.

Of all the family, only Alter and his mother returned from the evacuation. His father and sister had died in Uzbekistan, in the village not far from Urgench where they'd landed during the war, and his two older brothers had been fortunate to leave for Brazil in time to save their lives. Before the war, his mother, Soreh Serebrinski, had never been out of Alexăndreni. Now in Kishinev she had trouble adjusting to the big city. With a joke or a wise-crack, Alter would correct the clumsy Russian she spoke only when she had to. From time to time, he gently suggested how she could keep house the way the city people did. She did change, but only a little. Who could blame her? "Mother," Alter ended up saying, "do what you've always done, and if someone doesn't like it, too bad." After he got married, Adel set up the household according to her big-city tastes, but she not only gave the old woman her own room but allowed her to run the kitchen as she pleased. Adel was wise enough to treat her mother-in-law with respect, and the arrangement worked out well. In the evenings, when Adel came home from work tired, she found the house neat and clean and a good dinner waiting. Soreh Serebrinski wanted nothing to do with the special city dishes; from her kitchen you'd get soup with either noodles or buckwheat groats—always delicious. She'd been raised on soup, she said, the only girl out of seven children in the family. Her father was in the egg business. He and his sons worked from early in the morning till late at night loading the boxes of eggs, and she and her mother cooked 730 soups a year, two a day, for lunch and dinner, to feed the men. From helping her mother, she learned to cook, bake, and keep house—everything a woman needed to know.

At the end, when Soreh Serebrinski entered her final illness and only skin and bones remained of her once stout figure, she turned up her nose at the delicacies that Alter went to great lengths to obtain for her. "You want me to eat this?" she said. "All my life, all I ever wanted was a bite of grated radish and onion with chicken fat. And now—"

A day before her death, when a neighbor came to borrow her noodle board, she reminded her never to set a bottle of oil on the board, or it would leave a greasy stain.

As was the custom in those days, the coffin was placed on an open truck bed and the mourners followed behind on the way to the cemetery. As he walked, Alter kept looking at the wreath his coworkers at the MoldauFrTorgTekstil had sent to show their respects. He couldn't tear his eyes away from the wreath as it swayed back and forth on top of the coffin. In his mind's eye he saw his mother, who despised insincerity, rising up out of her coffin, hurling the "bunch of old twigs" onto the ground, and lying back down again.

When the others sitting on the bench hear this, they exchange glances.

"What can I do?" Alter says, "This is who I am, and this is who I will be to the end of my days. I always find something comic in a tragic situation, and vice versa. Not long ago," he went on, "we were at the funeral of a close acquaintance, a prominent person in town. You were there, too, Benderski. A relative of the deceased, a person who liked to hear himself talk, decided it would be a great honor for him to chant the *moley* prayer for the dead before such a big, impressive crowd. But he was very nervous, and instead of saying '*El moley rakhmim* shoykhen *ba-meroymim*,' he said, '*El moley rakhmim* yoyshev *ba-meroymim*.' I was shocked. I looked around to see how people were reacting, but they didn't even seem to notice."

"I don't understand, Alter," Benderski says. "What was so terrible?"

"Now here, Benderski," says Serebrinski, "we see the difference between a native of Kishinev and a native of Alexăndreni. You don't care whether it's 'God full of mercy who *dwells* in the heavens' or 'God full of mercy who *sits* in the heavens.' For you, it makes no difference whether the Lord of the Universe floats, sits, or stands on His head. You don't even listen. To you it's all the same. For those of us from Alexăndreni, however, it's another story entirely. If you insist on standing in the pulpit, then please be so good as to get it right. Otherwise, among my kind, you'll never live it down. Don't push your way into a place where you don't belong. You know ..."—and he continued as he always did, smoothly proceeding from one story to the next without allowing anyone to get in a word edge-wise—"here in town, at the local cemetery, there's a certain cross-eyed fellow, I'm sure you've seen him, the one with the bushy beard. I don't know his official position in the burial society, but he has a tight monopoly over the place, and even if you bring your own person to say the *moley*, he shows up too, and even though all he does is listen, you're expected to pay him anyway. This fellow, if you listen carefully, pronounces it '*el moley* rakheymim' instead of '*el moley* rakhmim.' I don't know about you, but to me it grates on the ears, yet no one speaks up. I'm afraid I'll have to be the one to take him on."

"How did you notice that?" Benderski says. "You're extraordinary!"

"Please, Benderski, don't play the fool," Serebrinski responds. "We've seen what you yourself are capable of. You earned your place in the world to come with your 'Sir Walter.' No one could possibly top that. I don't believe you have no small-town blood in you. You must have a grandfather, a grandmother, an aunt once removed—someone, somewhere. Otherwise you could never have come up with such a name."

Benderski takes the pipe out of his mouth and smiles, and everyone goes home in good humor.

3. THE SIMPLE CHILD: YANKEV BORISOVITSH

Yankev Borisovitsh is the simple child on "Benderski's bench"—a simple child with a university education and the title of "Doctor of Philology." How can this be? Here in Israel, anything is possible. He is indeed a doctor of philology, but having arrived in this country a scant three years ago, he understands only a smattering of Hebrew. Learning a language is difficult at his age—to him it all sounds like gibberish and goes in one ear and out the other. But he's determined to make progress, and whenever he has a free moment he sits down with his textbooks and dictionaries and applies himself to the task. The minimal proficiency he's managed to acquire so far, though, is not nearly enough to satisfy his scholarly ego. The whole thing drives him crazy. He can't imagine why a philologist like himself, with a reputation at the Moldovan Academy of Sciences in Kishinev, should find it so hard. It's true, though—he's not getting any better. So whenever possible he takes comfort in talking about the past. He talks and talks about how it was "back there," and since "there" in Russian is pronounced "*tam*," the same as the Hebrew word for "simple," the members of the group have attached the word to him—*Yankev Tam*, Yankev the Simple. Yankev Borisovitsh doesn't actually answer to the name—first because people tend not to use it to his face, and second because even when they do, he doesn't understand enough Hebrew to get the joke.

The bench in Elisheva Garden, "Benderski's bench," is the best thing that could have happened to him. He can ask the group about local laws and customs he has trouble understanding and about words and expressions he can't make sense of. During the course of the day he jots things down in his notebook, and every evening when they get together he takes this *seyfer khesroynes*, as he calls it, his "Book of Problems," out of his pocket, and there on the bench are people who can explain not only what

the words mean but also their etymology and other words
that stem from the same root. It's better than the language
classes he attended at the *ulpan*. This is the first benefit of
the bench.

There's another benefit, too. Sitting there with the others, he forgets all his troubles, all the various difficulties
and the associated family quarrels. Back in Moscow, where
they lived for many years, and later in Kishinev, the family
always got along well, but here everyone is always at odds.
Materially they're not doing badly. The rent does seem to
eat up practically the entire budget, but one mustn't complain—everyone else is in the same situation. The children
have found jobs more or less in their fields—his son at a
computer company and his daughter-in-law, for now, at a
hospital—so both of them are bringing in something on
top of their benefit checks. His wife, with her years of teaching experience, earns a good salary taking care of two little
children, and he works part-time as a guard at the local
supermarket. Day after day he sits by the door inspecting
people's bags. It's not much of a job, but what else can he
do? His area of expertise, Russian language and literature,
is worth nothing here, especially at his age. He doesn't
much enjoy the work, of course, and it's hard to get used
to people yelling "Ya'akov! Ya'akov!" from across the room
and bossing him around as if he were an errand boy. But all
this is nothing compared to the mistrust, the bad feelings,
and the painful quarrels that keep breaking out within the
family over things that make no difference whatsoever.

It was a stroke of good fortune that he happened to run
into his former neighbor, Alter Serebrinski, known here
as Sir Walter, who slowly drew him out of his melancholy.
Alter spoke bluntly. "There's no going back, my friend," he

said. "*Yo'q!*—no—as the Uzbeks say. Just stick it out, and you'll see, you'll make it through these problems—temporary ones, let's hope. We've all been through it in one way or another. It's like the chicken pox or the measles—everyone gets it, no matter how smart you are, and the older you are the worse it is. The only remedy is to smile, to laugh. Laugh through your tears if you have to. It's the only way to get over the 'illness.'"

He gave an example: "We had a relative here in the city, a pharmacist," he began, "and I never knew whether to laugh or cry over his situation. You know how pharmacists think the world of themselves—why, I don't know. They all believe they're the reason the world rotates around its axis, and they consider themselves too good to associate with anyone else. Even after death, you'll notice that the tombstone of a pharmacist always has his name inscribed in big letters in honor of his great wisdom—or at any rate, his great self-regard. Anyway, this relative of ours had done quite well here from the start. He received a good pension as a wounded war veteran and generally had a good life, but he was completely wrapped up in himself, had no friends, and never exchanged a word with a soul. He walked his big dog twice a day, and that was it.

"One time I couldn't help myself. 'What's your problem, man?' I asked him. 'Are you the only educated person in Israel? You think you know it all and everyone else is an idiot? God knows there are others who know just as much as you do, who can read a newspaper and even a book, who like a good game of chess—and yet you don't see them going around with their noses in the air the way you do. Why not try to meet other people, say hello, even have a conversation once in a while?'

"'Never in my life,' he answered proudly, 'have I sat on a park bench. I have neither the time nor the inclination.'

"'Well, well,' I responded. 'Are you suggesting that I've spent my life sitting on benches? As a matter of fact, I used to go to work at dawn and not come home till after dark. How could I have sat on benches? I used to fall asleep at the table. Fool that I was, I thought I'd be rewarded for my devotion. They'd build a beautiful tombstone in my honor, maybe. Oh, yes. And you see where it all got us. We ran around following orders, trying to catch up with America and overtake her. We were so brainwashed with all those empty promises and conformist thoughts that even now, in our old age, when we've been let off the leash, we're still at the mercy of those false dogmas that are engraved so deeply in our consciousness. But why,' I asked him, 'am I explaining all this to you?'

"Not long after," Alter went on, "my relative passed away. They had a terrible time finding a minyan for the funeral. His widow had the symbol of medicine engraved on his tombstone, and you could read the inscription from a mile away: 'Here lies the pharmacist Mordkhe Lemberg, son of Avrom, may he rest in peace.' He was a pharmacist, you see, not just anybody. She always had a very high opinion of him."

＊ ＊ ＊

One day Yankev Borisovitsh arrives in the park, takes out his "Book of Problems" as always, puts on his glasses, and starts in on the word *kholile*, or in its Israeli version, *halilah*, which means, as he knows from back home, "God forbid." So far, so good. Lately, however, he's been running into the expression *ve-hozer halilah,* which seems to mean something else entirely.

"Eh … Reb Ya'akov," Alter breaks in, "I see you've finished with the Five Books of Moses and now you're advanced enough for a page of Talmud commentary. Good for you! There are people who live here for decades without noticing the distinction you've put your finger on. You deserve to be congratulated. And now for the matter at hand. The point is that among us Jews, and maybe among others as well, not only the word itself but the pronunciation is important—specifically, the question of where the emphasis falls. With the expression *ve-hozer halilah,* for example, the stress belongs not on the second syllable, as in the word *kholile,* which, as you say, you know from back home, but on the last syllable, like this, *hali*lah. The difference in pronunciation, my friend, gives the word an entirely different meaning. *Ve-hozer halilah* means 'it repeats itself,' or in other words, 'and so on and so forth.'"

Benderski takes his pipe out of his mouth, then replaces it—a sure sign of annoyance. "Always first to jump in, that Alter," he thinks. "You can't hold him back. Before you can open your mouth, he's got the answer." And not to be outdone, Benderski himself tells a story from when he came to this country in 1972. He already knew the language well and had no particular trouble with it, yet he almost ruined his career over a single word.

"One word?"

"Over one word." Having managed for the moment to divert attention from his eternal rival, the Omniscient One, he feels better. "Over one word," he repeats, to prolong the pleasure. "The word *kedilkaman.* Go ahead, laugh. I can laugh now too, but back then I'd never heard of this word, not in all my years of Jewish education, and here it showed up everywhere, on every document and every form. It seemed no one could get by without it. Who knows, I thought, maybe it's a very important word derived from the Aramaic. Maybe everyone can tell how smart you are by the way you use it. I had no one I could ask who wouldn't laugh at me. I was worried sick. I didn't want to turn down the job I'd been offered, but at the same time I was scared to death that this *kedilkaman* would get me into big trouble. It got so bad that my Sheyndele noticed something was wrong.

"'Why are you so upset, Avreyml?' she said. 'Did you dream about the three windows on Minkovsky again?'

"'No, Sheyndele, it's not the windows, it's *kedilkaman*.'

"'What *kedilkaman*?' She was scared. 'What are you babbling about? Have you lost your mind?'

"'I don't know what *kedilkaman* means,' I said. 'I have no idea when and how to use it. How can I even think of taking that job?'

"My Sheyndele, as you know, is no babe in the woods. You don't need to explain things twice to her—she's from Odessa. The next day, when she came home from work, she was laughing so hard her double chin was shaking. She said, 'It's just as I thought—stuff and nonsense. If you want to use this word, be my guest. If not, you can get along perfectly well without it. Now listen to me. *Halan* means "what I already said," and *kedilkaman* means "what I'm about to say." Understand? The whole thing doesn't amount to a hill of beans. It's a lot of fuss over nothing."'

Everyone cheers. "*Molodets, baba!*" they cry—well done, woman!

The story has put them in a good mood. Yankev Borisovitsh raises his hand.

"All right, gentlemen, listen to this," he says. "I, too, have a story about a word—or should I say a name—and what matters is not so much the name itself as the way it was said—or in this case sung or shouted. When we lived in Kishinev, some Gagauz families lived down the street from us. Gagauz are a mixture of Turks and Bulgarians—some say they're more Turkish and some say they're more Bulgarian, I've never figured it out exactly. Anyway, they like a drink no less than the Moldovans or the Russians, especially on Sunday, their day of rest. One Sunday afternoon my wife and I were getting ready to go to the cinema. We'd put on our coats but we couldn't leave—the music on the radio was so enchanting. It was "Maria," sung by someone famous, I can't remember who. It wasn't a song, it was a prayer, a paean to Maria in both her heavenly and her earthly forms. Finally we turned off the radio and went out, still entranced by that voice—it was like velvet! Suddenly, a Gagauz woman pops out of the house next door like a cork out of a bottle. Her shawl is flying out behind her, her feet barely touch the ground, and after her comes her husband, dead drunk, barely able to stand, and he picks up a rock and throws it at her.

"'Ma-ri-a-a-a-a!' he roars. 'Ma-ri-a-a-a-a ...!'—followed by a string of obscenities.

"Maria again! My wife and I look at each other and burst out laughing, and then we go off to the movies arm in arm."

Benderski loves the story. "For that, Reb Yankev, you deserve a prize."

"You can just call me Ya'akov, like at the supermarket."

"There they can call you whatever they want, although it wouldn't hurt if they asked you first. But to us you're Reb Yankev."

"'Reb,' eh? What am I, a rabbi?"

"A doctor doesn't deserve a title?"

Yankev Borisovitsh happily puts his Book of Problems back in his pocket. It's getting dark, time to go home.

"One more thing," Alter Serebrinski says suddenly. "I've been meaning to ask—you were still in Kishinev three years ago, so you must know. You know the little house at the end of our street, where you turn to go to the Ilinsky market—the peasant cottage? I've been wondering—is it still there, or has it been torn down?"

"Torn down," says Yankev. "Right before we left, they knocked down a whole row of houses, and that cottage was one of them. They were clearing the way for a big new building."

"What a shame," says Alter. "That cottage was one of a kind, there was nothing like it in the whole region. Every year, for the First of May and again for the anniversary of the October Revolution, they'd give all the houses and fences a coat of yellow or green paint, and they'd always paint that cottage, too, dilapidated as it was. The paint would stick to the flaky surface like face powder on an old woman. Torn down, you say? That cottage wasn't far from the house where Pushkin lived when he was exiled to Kishinev. There's a museum there now. I wouldn't be surprised if that cottage goes all the way back to Pushkin's time. Who knows, maybe it was the model for the House on Chicken Legs in the fairy tale. Whenever I went by there, I used to wonder if it was about to rise up on its chicken legs—thatched roof and tiny windows and all—and turn its back on me, just like in the story. Torn down, you say? Just like that! What a pity!"

And they all go home feeling that everything is temporary, that nothing lasts forever, and that something very important has been lost.

4. THE FOURTH CHILD, WHO KNOWS NOT HOW TO ASK

Pavel Davidovitsh was the fourth child on the bench. He had many questions and he did know how to ask, yet he rarely spoke. In the first place, by nature he was a quiet man who preferred to listen. And years ago, he'd paid a heavy price for asking an innocent question. For that minor error, he'd gone through hell in the Ekibastuz camp in Kazakhstan. If he hadn't been young and healthy, he would never have survived those ten years of hard labor in the mines. There, in the underworld, he was stripped forever of the desire to open his mouth. An unasked question remained frozen inside him: Why did this happen to me?

Since coming to Israel, however, he has benefited from the sun, known for its ability to melt a stone, and from the group in the park, which keeps him from losing heart and helps him take things in stride in his old age. Here no one is surprised by anyone's troubles. Most people, both the native-born and the immigrants, have been through hard times. They've learned to cope with difficulties and sometimes to overcome them. Pavel Davidovitsh, or Pal for short, feels himself beginning to thaw, and from time to time he even finds himself wanting to talk about his past. The members of the group are glad to listen.

Pal Davidovitsh has a very sad life story. He never knew his mother, who died before he was a year old. His one image of his father is of a body lying on the floor covered in black, and people coming in and patting him, Pal, on the head. Other than that, nothing. His first clear memories are of the children's home for orphans of the Revolution, children abandoned and battered by fate. There he was called Pavlik. Most boys at the home were called either "Kesha," short for Innokenti, or "Pantile," for Panteley, and more than once Pavlik was singled out for a beating, because within those drab gray walls his name sounded a little too tender. Later, he learned from the administration that his name was Pavel Davidovitsh Tkatsh, that he was of Jewish nationality, and that he was born in 1916 in the town of Chechelnyk, in Vinnytsia Oblast. When he turned fourteen, the oldest allowed at the children's home, he was discharged. Armed with his personal data, his grammar school diploma, and his Komsomol card, he set off for Kiev to begin an independent life.

It was the early 1930s, when a terrible famine raged through all of Ukraine. The peasants in the villages had devoured their last stores of grain and their bellies were swollen with hunger, yet with their last strength they held onto their land and resisted joining the collective farms. Then the ruthless activist brigades arrived in all their "glory" to carry out the collectivization by force. Every last soul, along with every head of livestock, was driven into the *kolkhozes*. Those who refused to go were stripped of their land and their possessions and deported to Siberia with their families. To carry out this "magnificent" campaign, the regime recruited a contingent of strong young men who could be counted on to do whatever was necessary.

Pavlik met all the criteria. He was a Komsomol member, tall and healthy, who looked older than his years and possessed a "crystal clear" life story, including one of the most important requirements for being promoted to a position of responsibility: no parents or relatives either inside or outside the country. He was given new clothes and three meals a day, and the whip was placed in his hand.

For three years, he took part in the persecution of the peasant farmers, the "enemies of the people," who were to blame, he'd been convinced, for the fact that he and others like him had grown up as orphans, never knowing a happy childhood. For three years, he observed the heartbreaking scenes that occurred when families were separated and people were driven from their ancestral homes. He believed he was fulfilling his obligation to his country. Only in this way, he felt, would evil and corruption be rooted out to make way for a new era of happiness and freedom. He rose through the ranks and was awarded a position on the municipal council of the Communist Youth.

Then came 1936, the year of the terrible purges, when again and again the cadres were culled to eliminate the slightest trace of suspicious elements. It was enough to point a finger at someone—by the next day he would be gone. You became afraid of your own shadow and avoided saying hello to your neighbors and acquaintances—tomorrow any one of them could be locked up and you'd be under suspicion for associating with the enemy. You pulled your cap down over your eyes so that you couldn't see anyone and no one could see you.

Pavlik was confident he had nothing to worry about. He was sure he stood safely outside the circle of questionable citizens—until one day he was astonished to find himself smack in the middle of that circle. Before him stood the investigator, spewing venom.

"Can't stop shooting your mouth off, eh, Tkatsh?" he spat. "Starting to have doubts about the Party, are you?"

It was then that Pavlik asked his fateful question.

"What am I accused of? What do you suspect I—"

"Shut your trap, son of a bitch!" came the answer. "I ask the questions here. Do I make myself clear?"

"Yes, sir."

In the Ekibastuz camp, Pavlik felt he was being punished not so much for sins against his country—of that he believed himself innocent—as for his persecution of innocent people, for which he felt terrible pangs of conscience. Even after serving his term of hard labor, in his own eyes he hadn't atoned for those sins. To this day, scenes from his youth torment him at night. He wakes up screaming, and his wife Sima—his second wife, that is—can't calm him down. Fanny, his first wife, had lived through the same hell; they'd met on the day of liberation, on their way back home. She knew what to do in the middle of the night. She'd take his head in her hands, hold him close, and rock him until he fell asleep in her arms. Fanny . . . Feygele, his little bird, had flown away, leaving him with a wounded heart that he carried with him always. He'd seen her for the first time at the train station, wearing a big embroidered Pashtun shawl and a gray scarf knotted over her jacket. She was carrying a pack and counting out coins at the ticket window. He heard her give her name as Feyge Glikman, and without thinking he turned and asked if she was Jewish.

"I am. Why?"

"I'm Jewish, too," he said. "Pavel Davidovitsh Tkatch. I just got out and have no one to go home to."

"I'm not sure I'll find anyone alive in Bender," she said, "but I have to try."

"Bender—where is that?"

"In Bessarabia, near the Dniester River."

"Shall we go together?"

Feygele looked up in surprise. For a moment she was silent, as if consulting with someone in her head. Then she shrugged.

"All right," she said, "let's try it."

In the course of the journey, their two bundles became one, and of course Pavlik carried it and didn't allow Feygele to touch it. At every station he was the first to jump down to fill their pot with hot water. When he was lucky, he found some dry bagels at the concession, and then they enjoyed a feast fit for a king. He wouldn't even allow her to wash the dishes, but gladly did them himself. Feygele felt like a cherished bride whose every whim is anticipated and indulged. She took off her shawl and combed her hair before a little shard of a mirror, made two braids and coiled them on her head like a laurel wreath. After all the years of hard labor, loneliness, and despair, she began to feel like a woman again.

Within several days they grew more comfortable with each other, and Pavlik told her his story, concealing nothing and feeling a great relief. She too poured out her bitter heart. She grew up free as a bird in Bender, she said, close to the Dniester, on the side then belonging to Romania. Having no problems of her own, she found herself beginning to care about the world at large. She was thrilled by the news arriving from the Soviet side about the happy life based on justice for all and friendship among peoples. One dark night, her friend Sasha, an ardent communist, convinced her to swim across the border. The two of them were strong swimmers and expected to reach the shore safely. But halfway across, the Soviet guards caught sight of them and started shooting. Both of them dove under-water. Sasha drowned and Feygele swam to shore with her last strength. It was 1936. The Russian border patrol in Tiraspol didn't believe a word she said about wanting to be part of the Soviet cause and immediately turned her in to the NKVD. She was accused of being a spy, and so on and so forth . . .

When they reached Bender, she learned that of her whole family, only her brother-in-law had survived. He turned over to her two rooms in the family house, which by some miracle was still standing. There they began a new life, there their two sons were born, and from there, after a long, difficult illness, Pavlik escorted his Feygele to her eternal rest. He'd met his second wife, Sima, shortly after immigrating to Israel. She was a good woman, honest and respectable, and he had nothing against her, but . . . she wasn't Feygele. He couldn't turn his soul inside out for her, as the Russians say. She knew he'd served ten years, and this proved no impediment to the match. After all, who in the Soviet Union hadn't been in prison? But he never talked to her about his agonizing guilt, his sign of Cain. Not a word. And so he managed, everything was all right—*beseder,* as we say in this country.

The members of the group are silent, lost in thought. You can live out your life on God's green earth and no one will even imagine the heavy burden that presses on you and sometimes drags you under.

"Listen to me, Fayvl," says the chairman. He takes the pipe out of his mouth. "All of us are sinners, some more and some less. Believe me, in this land of ours, the Holy Land, if you give anyone a good shake, plenty of wrongs will tumble out, plenty of sins, plenty of youthful transgressions. You, Pal Davidovitsh, are no worse than anyone else, and you've atoned enough. The Lord will forgive you."

"Eh ... dear friend, if only I could believe you!" says Pal. "You know, there are times when I envy *them*, the ones on the other side. They have connections they can call on, people they can turn to for help if need be."

"Cold comfort!" says Benderski. "Forget about that. A person must be self-reliant, and I'm not saying that because I believe in Lenin, God forbid! It's common sense, that's all. But to each his own beliefs. Anyway, enough philosophy. This reminds me of a story. Maybe you've already heard it, maybe not, it doesn't matter. It must have been a good thirty years ago. In the month of Elul, as usual a group of Hasidim came from America to pay their respects to the memory of their *tsadik*, their leader, by saying a prayer at his graveside in Uman, in Ukraine. This time, on the way home, they stopped off in Kishinev with the idea of davening there during the Days of Awe. We were walking down the main street, right where Prospekt Lenina crosses Sinadinovska—you know, by the Central Telephone and Telegraph building. Suddenly the door opens and out comes a group of young guys with their beards and side curls, and their fur hats trimmed with sable, and their long black silk coats with the braided belts, and their white stockings with the beautiful black slippers, the likes of which are never seen in Russia. What

in the world? Everyone on the street stops to stare and
listen to them jabber.

"'They must be artists,' people decided, 'a new ensemble of singers and dancers.' But who were they and where
had they come from? No one had ever seen such costumes—except me. I knew who they were, but I didn't
say a word. Not that I was embarrassed or ashamed—I
just didn't want to call attention to myself. Today I would
have handled it differently. So then here's what happened.
You know the jewel of Kishinev, the famous Komsomol
Lake. Well, the group decided to go to the lake to perform *tashlikh*. By the Russian calendar, it was an ordinary
Wednesday. The guard is standing at his post as usual,
keeping order. Suddenly he sees this group sneaking
down to the lake, emptying their pockets, throwing something into the water. He leaves his post and goes running
over. He gives a smart salute and demands to know who
they are and where they're from.

"'We are Bratslaver Hasidim,' they answer. 'We came
from America to visit the grave of our leader in Uman.'

"'Bratslaver Hasidim' means nothing to him, but
America and Uman, these he knows. Oho, he thinks to
himself, fat carp have fallen into my net!

"'Then what are you doing in Kishinev?' he asks. 'And
why are you polluting our lake? What did you throw in
the water?'

"'Our sins,' they reply in Russian. To the guard, the
words sound somehow mocking.

"'Is that so?' he says. 'And you laugh and make fun of
me while I stand at my post and fulfill my duty to my
country. Come with me to the police station. We'll sort
this out there.'"

They've heard the story before, but they laugh heartily anyway. Pal, hearing it for the first time, laughs with them.

"I see those young guys around," says Pal, "with their side curls and their long coats. They stand there counting the leaves of a *lulav* for Sukkos before they'll buy it. What's the point? What difference does it make?"

"How can you ask such a thing?" someone answers. "Counting those leaves, obeying all those rules, is what has preserved us as a people over the generations, and with God's help it's what will enable us to see our righteous Messiah, *bimheyre beyemeynu*, speedily in our days, amen!"

"But it's almost the end of the twentieth century!"

"You're referring to progress in the field of technology, am I right?" says Sir Walter, who's been uncharacteristically quiet. "Be aware, Pal Davidovitsh, that there's no conflict whatsoever between progress and faith. Quite the contrary."

"How is that?"

"Very simple," says Sir Walter. "In Alexăndreni, for example, before Yom Kippur, pregnant women would perform the Yom Kippur ritual of *shlogn kapores*, using a chicken, of course, but also an egg. Why? Because just as they couldn't predict what would hatch from the egg, a hen or a cock, they also didn't know what kind of baby would be born, a boy or a girl. Today, however, thanks to modern technology, we have the ultrasound, and before a woman is even showing, she already knows what kind of baby she's carrying. In this way, you see, the question of the *kapores* is solved, she knows exactly how to atone."

Pal Davidovitsh looks at Alter and can't figure out whether he's serious or pulling his leg.

"You don't really know our Sir Walter yet, do you?" says the chairman. "Well, it's high time you did."

And they all stand up smiling and head for home.

THE GROUP FALLS APART

No one expected the group to fall apart so quickly. As if they'd been given the Evil Eye, the end was sudden and sad. Not long before, the group had been thriving, its ranks even enlarged with a few newcomers from Kishinev, who hung on the old-timers' every word, considering it a privilege to spend time with people who knew the language and could give them helpful advice. Well, God saw that it was good—too good. He removed one of the cornerstones, and the building collapsed.

Without warning, Alter Serebrinski, who'd never complained of anything in his life, who was, to hear him tell it, completely healthy, suddenly suffered a severe heart attack. A few days later he had another, and then Alter was no more—*yo'q*, as he'd liked to joke in Uzbek, in memory of his years in the village near Urgench during the Second World War. Between the two heart attacks, he was still cracking jokes and telling stories from Alexăndreni, and when Benderski, frightened, came running to the hospital, Alter assured him from his sickbed that there was no reason for concern.

"It's nothing serious, Avreyml," he said. "I'm not dying. The Lord wanted to examine me, that's all, so He sent me a summons and called me in for questioning. Just as a precaution. A couple of angels from hell looked me over and rejected me. Lucky for me, I didn't measure up, so as you can see, they let me go." He smiled. "Don't worry, Benderski," he said. "With God's help, I'll be better in no time and, God willing, we'll keep on meeting as always in our Elisheva Garden. Take care of the group, don't let it break up."

The next evening he died.

Benderski was in shock. He couldn't sit still, couldn't sleep. Sheyndele brought him hot tea with lemon, laid compresses on his forehead, made him take a Lorivan. Nothing helped. All night he was wide awake, impatiently waiting for morning. Then he sprang into action. First he called an acquaintance who had a neighbor, a prayer leader with a wonderful voice, who agreed to recite the *moley* and read from the Book of Psalms. Money was no obstacle, he told him. Then he went to take care of the death notice and arranged for a copy to be posted at the entrance to the park. After that he hurried to the cemetery, where he tracked down the man Alter had talked about, the cross-eyed one with the bushy beard, and offered him a deal.

"Your fee is ten shekels? I'll give you twenty to stay away from the funeral."

The man accepted the offer on the spot, no questions asked. Benderski went away greatly relieved. He hadn't had to reveal that the deceased, may he rest in peace, had been highly critical of the man's *moley*. Such things it was better not to say. Nor had he had to tell a lie.

The funeral took place at three o'clock in the afternoon. Benderski stood by the grave, head bowed, listening to the *moley* as he had never listened before. He didn't miss a word. When the prayer was over, he said "amen" with everyone else. Then a deep sigh escaped from his chest. He took out his handkerchief and wiped his glasses. In a blur, he shook hands with the other mourners, and after they left he stayed behind.

"Alter ben Moyshe Serebrinski" read the marker, barely visible among the floral wreaths. "Ekh, Alterl," he said silently, "you won't be rising up like your mother Soreh Serebrinski, may she rest in peace, to fling those 'bunches of twigs' off your grave, but I'm sure you've been listening to every word. I played a dirty trick on you, as you used to say. I went looking for the very best prayer leader, especially for you, so that even the child prodigy from Alexăndreni wouldn't be able to find anything to complain about. Have you ever heard such a *moley*, Alterl? The very stones were weeping. Now you can rest peacefully in your bed, and as for everything else I've done, dear friend, forgive me."

Benderski never returned to Elisheva Garden. Once or twice he approached the fence, hid among the trees, and looked over at the bench, the one with his name on it, "Benderski's bench"—which had survived, as he well knew, only because of Alter Serebrinski. More than once he'd envied his friend's spark, the Alexăndreni light inside him that never went out. He felt sure that now, without that soul, that spark of life, the group could not last. Even if it did, it would never be the same.

The first time he went, from a distance he could see the orphaned friends bent over Yankev Borisovitsh's "Book of Problems," arguing endlessly as usual. The sight broke his heart. He hesitated, debating whether to go in, but at the last minute he made up his mind and turned away. For him the group was no more.

ERIKA

Arka, they say, was one of the founders of our town. For that reason he'd been given a generous plot of land, where he built himself a splendid two-story brick house. It had a big shop in front, bright, spacious rooms with all the conveniences, and a magnificent glassed-in veranda. After the house was finished, other people who were planning to build began stopping by with their architects to make sketches. Arka didn't mind, but after a while his wife, Zlata, had had enough. She suggested they go look at other houses, the ones already copied from Arka's. Zlata was not particularly nice, a bit snooty. Arka did his best not to take her on. When people came by, he'd send them straight to her. "Ask Zlata," he'd say with a smile, "she'll show you around." This is why he was known as Zlata's Arka. Or maybe he got the name because he was from

Poland and always reckoned the local currency in *zlotys*.
Anything is possible.

When I met him, he was pale and skinny and very old.
People addressed him as Reb Aron to his face, but called
him Old Man Aron behind his back. By that time, his
son, Avrom Sharfshteyn, was running the hardware store,
while his daughter-in-law Soreh looked after him as if he
were her own father. She kept him clean, served his meals
on time, and on sunny days took him out "for air," seating
him in a comfortable chair on the porch with a shawl over
his shoulders so people could see that he was enjoying a
good old age.

We lived nearby, and when I was young I was scared
of Reb Aron. I was afraid he'd topple out of his chair and
die just as I walked by and said hello. As I approached his
house, I'd slow down and take a look, and only if he was
sitting up straight would I keep going.

Sometimes, when I went for a walk, the rabbi's dog,
whose name was Bear, would stroll along in front of me.
In our town it was rare for Jews to own a dog—it was
considered un-Jewish. Dogs hung around the butcher
shop, snarling over the scraps. Some of the non-Jewish
government officials, such as the town treasurer and the
police inspector, also had dogs, so we avoided going past
their houses unless we had to. But a rabbi with a dog was
very unusual. Rabbi Bernshteyn had come to us from
Romania, though, where apparently they did things differently. The rabbi himself had nothing to do with the
dog; his sons did, along with his wife, who ran the household. She spoke Romanian to the dog as if to an equal.
When a chicken escaped from its cage, she'd cry, "*Urs,
prinde găină*"—Bear, go get the hen—and Bear would

leap up, catch the chicken gently by one wing, and bring it to her, placing it in her hand. Bear understood several languages—Romanian, Yiddish, Hebrew, and a few words of Russian, including *poshel von,* beat it. He was a highly educated dog, lively and intelligent, a scholar. He knew he wasn't a guard dog—the rabbi didn't own anything worth protecting—and he understood that when people came to the rabbi for advice there was no point in barking at them. Things were bad enough for them already, so he left them alone. But even though he did nothing to scare them, they were afraid anyway. People were like that, he found; even if you didn't go near them, they were on their guard, spoiling for a fight.

One time, for example, he was walking along minding his own business. He stopped and nodded his head to say "Hello, Reb Aron, how are you today?"—upon which the old man, who was barely alive, turned and stamped his feet, whispering *"poshel von!"*

I ask you, Bear said to himself, is this any way for an intelligent person to behave? He regarded Reb Aron with pity. The old man had lost his wits, it seemed. What are you so excited about, mister? he wondered. Who could be afraid of you? Calm down and stop making a fool of yourself. I was brought up by a rabbi, you know, and he taught me a thing or two. So long, Reb Aron, I won't bother barking. And he continued on his way.

Soon afterward, Old Man Aron died. A year later, his granddaughter, who had married a doctor, gave birth to a girl, and they named her Erika after her grandfather. Doctors, you see, even when they name a child after a relative, change the name to something different. The town kept its mouth shut. Around here we don't argue with doctors.

✦ ✦ ✦

All this came to my mind decades later, here in Israel, when I bought myself an Erika brand typewriter on Nachlat Binyamin Street in Tel Aviv, where they sell antiques. The salesman was pleased, because in the computer age it's not easy to find a buyer for a typewriter. I was pleased, too, especially when I noticed the name Erika.

I don't know who the brand is actually named for, but as far as I was concerned it was in honor of the Erika from back home. I decided to turn the tables and call my new machine "Reb Aron."

"Please, Reb Aron," I say as I remove the oilcloth shawl from his shoulders, "would you be so kind as to walk with me through the streets and alleys of our destroyed town? There's almost nothing left back there, and people who don't know a thing about our past like to drag our name through the mud. They say it was all filth, poverty, and disease back then. How do you like that, Reb Aron? It's a good thing we came to Israel, don't you think? Otherwise we'd both be stuck there going senile."

Reb Aron looks at me and sighs. He wants to say something, but his voice doesn't work well enough anymore. His eyes are not in great shape, so I often wipe them for him. I keep his innards oiled, too, and once, when he came down with a touch of arteriosclerosis, I moved heaven and earth to find a geriatric specialist who could put him back on his feet.

People laughed at me when I bought the typewriter. It's not worth the trouble, they said. Get yourself a computer.

I didn't answer. But to myself, I said no. I don't always do what's most expedient. If only a small circle of Jews read Yiddish these days, does that mean I should stop writing in Yiddish? Yiddish is my language. In Yiddish I feel at home, younger, more at ease. If others choose not to understand, that's their problem. Even Bear understood that our people are always looking for something to fight about, and when we can't find anyone else to pick on, we go after our own.

He's my Reb Aron, and long may he live. Long may he look after my spirit, long may he awaken my memories, my yearnings, the rare tremblings of my soul, without which there would be no point in writing at all.

As for those who insist on mocking us and wishing us ill, no doubt our old cantor back home could have tracked down a passage from the Torah to shed light on the dispute. I will simply say this: As long as they bother to go after us, we can be sure we still exist.

THE SECOND TIME AROUND

In the middle of the night, Ella awoke with a start, frightened to death. Hailstones pounded on the shutters, threatening to smash them to pieces. The wind sounded as fierce as Ashmedai, king of the demons, and a loose pane in the hallway made the apartment door whistle and moan like a pack of jackals. The eight-story building seemed to rock back and forth, as if at any moment it would be torn off its foundation and carried out to sea. In a daze, she struggled to get up from the divan and knocked the screen onto her head.

Good God, what was happening? Down on her knees, she grabbed for the table and pulled herself up. She could die of fright right here on the floor and no one would even know. The electricity was out, possibly in the whole neighborhood. She couldn't see a thing.

For a moment she lost her bearings, then took herself in hand. She was no fragile flower, after all. She had lived a long life and knew how to take care of herself. She felt her way into the kitchen, found matches next to the stove, lit two candles and breathed a little easier. She filled two glasses with water and placed them in the windows, as her mother would have done. It might not be enough to make the hail stop, but it helped. No longer alone in the apartment, she had her mother with her now, and that was a comfort.

It was decades since her mother had died. Ella had long since surpassed her in age. Now a grandmother herself, she took every opportunity to talk to the grandchildren about her mother and what she used to say and do. Recently she'd been telling a neighbor what her mother used to say about Short Friday, the darkest Friday of the year. In her mother's view, only a lazy person would complain that Short Friday was so short that there wasn't enough time to prepare for Shabbos. To her mother, Short Friday was a good thing, because from that point on the days started getting longer. Each passing day, her mother used to say, was longer by exactly the amount of time it took for a rooster to jump onto a fence, flap its wings, and cry cock-a-doodle-do. Her mother knew everything, it seemed. She had an answer for every question, and every answer was full of Jewish wit and charm.

By now the hail had indeed stopped. Ella got back in bed, pulled up the covers, and tried to sleep. But the thunder and lightning started up again, and the rain hammered mercilessly on the roof.

A flood! Evidently God had decided to destroy the world again. She got out of bed, put on her clothes, and gathered up a few things to take with her in case she needed to evacuate. Fully dressed, she draped a shawl over her shoulders and settled into the armchair to wait for morning. There she fell asleep.

It was broad daylight when the telephone rang. The sun was shining bright and clear on a fresh-washed world, displaying her dazzling rays as if to show that she had had nothing to do with the events of the night before. The sun held herself apart from the other forces of the cosmos. Of them all, she alone had the power to console the lonely, the desperate, the sad.

Ella had no idea where she was as she opened her eyes. She picked up the phone and said hello in a sleepy voice.

"Elkele! Good morning!"

"Good morning, Naum. Why are you calling so early?"

"It's not so early. I waited till seven. I heard on the radio about the flood in Haifa. They say the wind caused a lot of damage. I had to call and see how you survived all by yourself."

"I almost didn't," Ella said. "But as you can hear, thank God I made it. I guess it all worked out for the best."

"So it did," he said. "How do they put it—sometimes a little bad luck does the trick better than good fortune. A night like that can lead a person to make a big decision, am I right, Elkele? But let's talk about that another time, under more favorable conditions. Maybe face to face. Right now I'm just glad to hear your voice and know you're all right."

✦ ✦ ✦

All day Ella couldn't stop thinking about the nightmarish storm and the phone call that had awakened her and brought her back to life. Yes, back to life! His calling her Elkele the way her parents did and his concern about how she'd gotten through the dreadful night felt like a sudden beam of light shining in the darkness. After her husband's tragic death, she'd been alone for so many years, so busy making a living and helping with the grandchildren, that she hadn't given much thought to herself. The time passed quickly, and she was glad. Soon enough it would all be over for her, and she didn't really mind. She'd made peace with her situation and had neither the strength nor the desire to change. It was no easy matter to start over again in old age, to get used to a new person, to adapt to his habits, his whims. She'd driven such thoughts from her mind and rebuffed the proposals that came her way. She would remain alone, alone and pure. Yet every Saturday morning she found herself getting out of bed and hurrying to the window to wait for "the couple." No matter how many times she vowed to give up the foolish game, the compulsion was stronger than she was. What it was all about she couldn't explain even to herself. It was easy to spy on people from the eighth floor. You didn't even have to hide behind the curtain. You could see everything, and no one could see you.

She had discovered "the couple" only recently. Every Shabbos the scene played out like a silent film, and she tried never to miss a showing. She already knew the plot, and the two protagonists were always the same, yet every week there were new details that sent her imagination off in new directions. The man was very old but still carried himself like an aristocrat. His sensitivity and high culture could be seen in his slender figure, his refined features, and especially his delicate hands. His beautifully tailored suit and matching brown hat exuded wealth and good taste. Even his cane looked expensive. His glasses, though, with their tinted bifocal lenses, suggested that his vision was failing. Every week the woman guided him to the synagogue across from Ella's building. She helped him cross the street, then waited for the *shames* or someone from the congregation to come out and help him up the steps. After that she sat down on a bench and waited till she was sure he was safely inside, and then she stood up and started for home. Like him, she carried herself with dignity. At 11:00 on the dot she returned to the bench, and when the service ended and people started coming out of the synagogue, she crossed over and took his arm, and off they went.

The question was this: Was she his wife or just a caretaker? Surely not his caretaker. A woman with such a beautiful face would never end up as a servant to such a man. More likely his wife, and probably they'd married late in life. The second time around, so to speak. If the first wife were alive, she wouldn't be turning herself inside out to meet his every need. After taking care of him for years, she'd be standing up for her rights by now.

"You want to make up with God in your old age?" she'd say. "Fine, but leave me out of it." With the second wife it would be different. Inside, she could think whatever she wanted, but outwardly she'd have to hold her counsel and bend to his wishes more than she might prefer.

Ella was not proud of these harsh observations. Sour grapes, she scolded herself. If she herself hadn't had the sense to find a partner while there was still time, that gave her no right to hold herself above anyone else. Was it so terrible for the other woman to try to relieve the loneliness that was so hard to bear on Shabbos and holidays? Today Ella had watched the woman straighten the man's collar and tuck a handkerchief in his pocket, and he had patted her hand. The wild billy goats you saw kissing and pawing at each other in the streets these days would never understand the tenderness of that caress.

❖ ❖ ❖

On Shavuos, Naum arrived for a two-day visit. Ella had hesitated before agreeing to let him come. It wasn't an easy decision. She'd worried about how the children would take it, and worse yet, the grandchildren, who would probably think Grandma had lost her mind. Old people didn't get married, did they?

Her daughter calmed her down and gave her courage.

"Enough, Mama," she said. "You've spent enough time alone." She knew what it was like, she said, she'd been through it herself. Ella had sacrificed enough for the children, and now it was time to think about herself, before it was too late. "Who knows you the way I do, Mama?" Of course it would have been hard to get together with a total stranger, but here was someone from her own hometown. That would make it easy to get along with him, even in old age. Besides, they'd been corresponding. "Believe me," she said, "if you hadn't liked his letters, you wouldn't have stuck around."

Naum looked good, smartly dressed with a bouquet of flowers in his hand and a song in his heart. He went straight to the bookshelf, which made Ella smile. Another attribute to add to the list. He was relieved, she could tell, not to have to struggle with an unfamiliar language;

instead he could relax into his own Bessarabian Yiddish with its juicy broad vowels. Ella's sorrel soup smelled just like his mother's, he said, and the bagels with cream cheese made a perfect Shavuos feast. Best of all, as soon as they finished eating he began to sing—not one of the traditional Sabbath songs but Leyvik's "Lay Your Head on My Knees." In Ella's heart, the verdict was signed and sealed, the decision made.

And then the Lord, the universal matchmaker on high, generously bestowed upon them a few hot, sunny days to warm their spirits and encourage them to enjoy life. They went to the beach.

The two of them had been born and raised in the same town, far from oceans or seas. All they had was a little stream known as Zhelinski's River, choked with moss, reeds, and grass. No sensible person would set foot in it for fear of leeches, worms, and other creatures. As a result, neither of them could manage much more than a dog-paddle. They took a brief dip, then sat on the warm sand exposing their not-so-young backs to the sun.

"We may not be big swimmers," Naum said, "but I'll tell you a story from ... well, it doesn't matter how many years ago. Do you remember Yankl from back home? The one we called 'the Bagman' because he was so good at repairing sacks? Yes, there were once such specialists among us back then. Remember the people who would bind clay pots with wire to keep them from falling apart, and the ones who could repair used clothing so that it was as good as new? Today, of course, you mention something like that to the children and they don't want to hear it. 'Not that old stuff again!' Anyway, this Yankl had a little brother about my age named Zelik, a little devil. When

I got my first tricycle from Kishinev, all the kids were jealous. One time, when I wouldn't let this Zelik have a turn on my new 'krike,' as he pronounced it, he decided to play a trick on me. The next day, when he saw me down by Zhelinski's River, he went running to my house screaming that I had drowned. Of course the whole town rushed down to the riverbank, and there I was, sitting on the bank, as innocent as a newborn babe, discussing an important matter with my best friend Yisroyl Skolnik.

"Zelik got a beating, but my desire to go near water was also beaten out of me. I've been a terra firma type ever since. What about you, Elkele, did you ever swim in Zhelinski's River?"

"Of course I did," Ella said. "The Volga was too far away, and besides, as you know, the Volga was the Russian river and Zhelinski's was the Jewish one, divided into two parts like a synagogue." The women and girls would bathe on one side, not in bathing suits but in their regular clothes, and on the other side, near the water wheel, there was a stronger current known as "the shower" where the men would splash around, naked as the day they were born.

"Everyone made fun of our pathetic little 'Volga,'" Naum said, "but on hot summer days, no matter how brown and rusty the water was, we couldn't stay away."

"The older you get," Ella said, "the more the memories bubble up, and you look at things in a different light. After everything we've seen and done, it seems, the best part is remembering the past."

"We had a neighbor," Naum said, still deep in the pleasure of recollection, "Itsik Shnayder, maybe you remember him. He used to talk to us about his father, who was always in motion. They called him 'Shmuel the Bird' because he was so lively and quick. He hated being idle, and he couldn't bear to see other people sitting around doing nothing either."

Eventually, Naum went on, Itsik's father, this Shmuel the Bird, fell gravely ill, and in keeping with custom, two members of the burial society arrived to sit by his deathbed and escort his soul into the other world. Suddenly he opened his eyes and saw them.

"Why are you just sitting there?" he asked in a weak voice.

"What should we do, Reb Shmuel?"

"Boil water!"

Even on his deathbed, Naum said, the man couldn't tolerate people sitting idle—they should be preparing the water to wash his corpse.

Ella had known this story ever since she could remember. They used to say it at home: Don't just sit there, boil water! Everyone, even the children, knew what it meant. But here they were in Haifa, on the magnificent beach with its pavilions and all its attractions, its half-naked young people noisily chasing one another and playing handball right over her head, as if they, the old couple, were in their way. Just to spite them, she burst out laughing, as if she were hearing the story for the first time.

Pleased to have amused her, Naum got up and went for ice cream. Ella took out her mirror, fixed her hair, and reapplied her lipstick. Then something made her turn her head. Nearby, two famished, lonely eyes were staring at her with a mixture of curiosity, envy, and perhaps a trace of scorn. What are you so happy about? they were saying.

What makes you so sure you'll get along with him in old age? How do you know you'll be good for each other?

When Naum returned with the sweet dessert, the woman stood up to go. One last question, the eternal, painful question, remained hanging in the air:

What makes you any better than me, and why do you deserve to be so happy?

About Yenta Mash

By Jessica Kirzane and Ellen Cassedy

In the story "Resting Place," Yenta Mash tells the story of
a group of Jewish women who have been sent into exile.
The women and girls have spent weeks crammed together
in stinking boxcars, infested with lice and deprived of
food and fresh air. Now they are confined to a slow-moving barge on the Ob River, embarked on a nauseating and
seemingly endless journey to a Siberian labor camp. Mash
does not hold back in describing the women's privations,
but as she does so, she lifts their devastating situation to
higher literary ground. In evocative and descriptive prose,
she explores how we make meaning out of traumatic and
brutal experiences.

Mash argues for the need to remake prayer and prose
anew, to speak to and uplift the grave traumas of the
twentieth century. When Shprintse, one of the deportees, recounts her dreams to the other women, the act of
storytelling lifts the women's spirits: "Everyone is all ears,
listening with pleasure and begging for more." Shprintse
not only satisfies her listeners' hunger for scenes from
back home but also embellishes and changes them. In so
doing, she creates a verbal picture that sustains her desperate audience. Through narrative, she gives the women
respite, even hope.

Later in the same story, Shprintse fosters creativity and
flexibility again as her young daughter Ester pronounces

prayers of mourning over a ninety-year-old woman who has perished during the harrowing journey. Traditionally, it is the job of men to perform burial rites. Without men, and without access to sources of authority on religious custom, the women are silent and anxious as they prepare the body, unsure if they are honoring the deceased with proper respect. Ester steps forward to recite the blessings, and when she stumbles and fails to use the Hebrew name of the dead woman, Shprintse reassures her that "it doesn't matter. If the Lord can allow us to be exiled to Siberia, then He'll have to learn some new languages, not just the holy tongue."

With her words, Shprintse admonishes a God who has allowed women to be sent into exile, away from the people and places that would have made it possible to carry out the burial according to every detail of Jewish tradition. Her words are also a nihilistic assertion that nothing matters, that ritual and religion are meaningless in the face of such suffering. At the same time, they are a call to creativity, asking Ester to remake the language of death and of holiness as she knows how. Shprintse gives permission to Ester to address God and the Jewish community in her own voice, speaking out of her trauma and her pain, because such acts of creativity are necessary for survival in the extreme circumstances in which the women find themselves.

This creative energy rings forth again and again in the work of Yenta Mash, which is available to English-language readers for the first time in this translation. Mash elevates and embellishes trauma to create beauty and meaning, drawing on tradition to reconstruct language and heritage in a new, female voice. Drawing on her own life, Mash offers an intimate perch from which to explore little-known corners of the twentieth and early twenty-first century. As a master chronicler of exile, Mash makes a major contribution to the literature of immigration and resilience, adding her voice to those of Jhumpa Lahiri, W. G. Sebald, Andre Aciman, and Viet Thanh Nguyen. Her protagonists are often in transit, poised "on the landing," on their way to or from somewhere else. She traces an arc across continents, across upheavals and regime changes, and across the phases of a woman's life from girlhood to old age.

YENTA MASH'S LIFE AND TIMES

Born Yenta Roytman on March 17, 1922, Mash grew up in Zgurița (Zguritse in Yiddish), a small town located in the region once known as Bessarabia. Today it lies within the nation of Moldova, just east of Romania. Growing up, she was steeped in the local Jewish culture with its distinctive regional pronunciation and idioms. She received both a Jewish and a secular education and trained and worked as a teacher.

As World War II loomed, this world was shattered as Soviet, German, and Romanian forces squeezed the region in a bloody grip. In 1941, when she was nineteen, Mash and her parents, along with other "bourgeois elements," were exiled to the Siberian gulag. There she endured years of hard labor under extreme conditions of hardship and hunger. Her father perished in a camp in the Ural Mountains, and her mother died in a forest in Siberia.

Released from the gulag in 1947, she married Michael Mash and settled not far from her girlhood home in the city of Chişinău (Kishinev in Yiddish), the site of the world-famous anti-Semitic pogrom of 1903, which had become the capital of the Moldavian Soviet Socialist Republic. For three decades she worked as a bookkeeper while recovering from the physical and psychological scars of her exile. She longed to write about her family, her childhood home, and her experiences in Siberia, but even speaking of this period was painful for her, and writing about her deportation could have been dangerous. Although she didn't write, she was an avid reader of Russian and world literature and was acquainted with Yiddish writers and journalists who were part of the thriving Jewish cultural life in the city, including Yekhiel Shraybman, her brother-in-law Yankl Yakir, and Motl Sakzier.

Mash's husband died in an automobile accident in 1971, and in 1977 she moved to Israel with her daughter's family and settled in Haifa. Here, in her fifties, she began to write and to publish, bringing to life a world that had been destroyed, the fragments of which she had left behind. In 1985 she married David Gurvits, a Yiddish cultural activist who encouraged her writing. She cultivated professional relationships and friendships with writers such as Mordechai Tsanin, Abraham Sutzkever, Rivka Basman Ben-Hayim, and Michael (Mishe) Lev. She was an active participant in the circle that met at Leyvik House, a Yiddish literary center in Tel Aviv, and the Association for Yiddish Writers and Journalists in Israel.

Mash's output was prodigious. From the start her work won praise—both for its high literary quality and for its documentation of the lost world of Jewish Bessarabia, the experiences of women in Siberia, the daily texture of life behind the Iron Curtain, and the challenges of assimilation in Israel. After her debut in the prestigious Tel Aviv journal *Di Goldene keyt*, edited by Abraham Sutzkever, Mash's short stories and essays were published in Yiddish-language journals on both sides of the Atlantic, among them *Letste nayes*, *Yerushalmer almanakh*, *Naye tsaytung*, *Toplpunkt*, *Vortbild*, and *Yisroel shtime* in Israel, and *Afn shvel*, *Tsukunft*, *Yidishe kultur*, and *Forverts* in America. Her writing received numerous prizes, including the Segal Prize for Yiddish Literature (1994), the Itsik Manger Prize (1999), and the David Hofshteyn Prize (2002). She died in Israel in 2013.

The sixteen stories in this collection are selected from Mash's four volumes of collected work: *Tif in der tayge* (*Deep in the Taiga*, 1990), *Meshane mokem* (*A Change of Place*, 1993), *Besaraber motivn* (*Bessarabian Themes*, 1998), and *Mit der letster hakofe* (*The Last Time Around*, 2007).

HISTORICAL CONTEXT

The Eastern European region once known as Bessarabia, where Yenta Mash was born, is bounded by the Dniester River on the east and the Prut River on the west. At different times, this borderland came under the control of different states and cultures. The earliest reference to Jews in the area dates from the fifteenth century, when small numbers of Jews, most of them engaged in commerce, settled in the region. At that time, the area was under the control of Hungary and Poland. Later it was subsumed by the Ottoman Turks, and during the Russo-Turkish War (1806–1812) it fell under Russian tsarist rule. At this point, the area became ethnically diverse, with the influx of Russian officials as well as Ukrainian, Bulgarian, German, and Jewish settlers.

Bessarabia was part of the Pale of Settlement established in 1791—the western part of the Russian Empire within which Jews were permitted to live. Jews ran mills, breweries, and inns. They were not allowed to own agricultural land, but some lived and worked in Jewish agricultural colonies established by tsarist authorities. Bessarabian Jews were Yiddish-speaking and mostly poor. The Jewish population in the region grew significantly in the 1800s, and population growth as well as economic pressures led to a rise in anti-Semitic sentiment in the region. The infamous May Laws of 1882 restricted Jews' economic activities for decades, and they fell victim to state-endorsed violence, including the 1903 Kishinev pogrom. By the late nineteenth century, however, the region had become a bastion of secular Hebrew education, Yiddish publishing, and religious and political activism.

In 1917, in the period of the Russian Revolution, Bessarabia briefly constituted itself as an autonomous Russian republic, but in early 1918 the Romanian Army intervened, and a parliamentary assembly declared it a part of the Kingdom of Romania. During the Romanian period (1918–1940), Jews suffered from significant state anti-Semitism, but at the same time they enjoyed some civil rights and ran autonomous schools and social-welfare institutions.

Under secret agreements included in the 1939 non-aggression pact between the USSR and Hitler's Germany, the

Soviet Union annexed Romanian-controlled Bessarabia in 1940. At that time there were more than 200,000 Jews in Bessarabia, representing over 7 percent of the population.

On June 14, 1941, as part of Soviet premier Joseph Stalin's policy of political repression against individuals deemed potentially hostile to the socialist regime, thousands of people were rounded up and deported to the gulag—a vast forced-labor system of camps situated throughout the Soviet Union. Although most of the deportees had committed no criminal acts and broken no laws, they were nonetheless designated as members of criminalized and marginalized sectors of the population. Among them were Jews who were considered capitalist property owners or advocates of Zionism. Deportation saved them from annihilation at the hands of Nazi forces, but the exile was harsh. The deportees were shoved into railroad cars, delivered to collection depots, and transported to prison camps across the USSR. Many died on their way to the unknown. Families were separated. The men were sent to labor camps in the Urals, while women and children were carried deep into the interior, to a land of frozen steppes, snowy forests, and surging rivers. Nineteen-year-old Mash and her parents were among these victims.

Just days after the deportations, on June 22, 1941, German and Romanian forces attacked Bessarabia. Many of the Jews who had been left behind after the deportations tried to flee under the intensive air bombardment. The Romanian regime ordered Jews to be incarcerated, deported by foot on death marches, and murdered en masse. An estimated 100,000 Bessarabian Jews perished during World War II.

After the war, the Jewish survivors who made their way back to the region found their homes and communities destroyed. The postwar Jewish population numbered fewer than 100,000 (3.3 percent of the population of the Moldavian Socialist Soviet Republic), less than half of the figure before the war. Jews struggled to come to terms with the loss of their prewar world and the consequences of their wartime suffering, and to deal with shifting Soviet rules that restricted freedom of religion and cultural expression.

In the 1970s, when emigration opened up for Soviet Jews, many Bessarabian Jews settled in Israel. Mash describes the cultural and generational challenges that she and her fellow immigrants experienced as their past receded into memory. With its emphasis on modern Hebrew as an official language, the Israeli state discouraged the use of Yiddish. Nevertheless, Mash pursued her literary endeavors as a member of a determined cadre of literary stalwarts who insisted that Yiddish culture would not end with the devastating events of the twentieth century.

ABOUT THE STORIES

Mash took seriously her responsibility to document the world that had been torn asunder in the 1940s. "Our former Bessarabia has lost its Jews and even its name," she wrote in the prologue to her second collection. Through her writing, she sought to add her own "colorful pebble to the mosaic" of cultural memory.

In the opening story, "The Bridegroom Tree," a Jewish survivor of Siberian exile returns to her ruined small town after World War II. Making her way through the weeds, she remembers the town's vibrant life before the war and the terrifying night in June of 1941 when she and thousands of others were rounded up by Soviet authorities. The story serves as an introduction to the shocking loss and horror that fill the stories that follow, and to the understated tone in which chaotic events will be described.

Varied in length and tone, the stories in this volume follow the trajectory of Mash's own life. The stories are not only about survival amid calamity but about the struggle to forge relationships in extreme circumstances, the importance and difficulty of recounting traumatic experiences, and the feelings of guilt and bewilderment that accompany efforts to carry on after desperate misfortune. As we read the stories together, they build upon and illuminate one another, so that each successive story feels more powerful because of the knowledge we have gleaned from those that come before.

Mash brings women's experiences to the fore, adding a fresh perspective on historical events that readers may know only through the eyes of male writers and their male characters. Young and old, her women characters adopt new roles and display resilience in response to new circumstances. Mash's intimate portrayal of life in the gulag demonstrates that it was not only a place of suffering but also a place of life, with real and complicated ties among women struggling to survive. Haunting and captivating, the stories focus on the day-to-day emotional and psychological toll of hunger and deprivation.

They grapple with social and political issues but are also intensely religious, very often invoking and questioning God's indifference.

In "Bread," the author discloses how her mother died in the forest while gathering food, but she buries that information mid-paragraph in an account of the experience of starvation, in which a crust of bread becomes the center of the universe, even more important than a mother. The story conveys multiple profound and bitter truths—the impossibility of talking about something as painful as a mother's death in the taiga, as well as the overpowering experience of hunger.

In "Alone," Galya, a Jewish prisoner in Siberia, draws upon her inner resources as she trudges through the snowy forest. The story opens with the surprisingly familiar and mundane thoughts of a teenage girl as she tries to entertain her mind and distract her freezing body. She smiles to herself at the comical image of two sweethearts trying to kiss each other with frozen lips and wonders what her admirers back home in Bessarabia would think of her rugged clothing. In these moments of calm, Mash reminds us of the humanity behind the suffering. Then the tale takes a dark turn, as Galya discovers a frozen corpse, struggles against death, and cries out against God's cruelty. Even though these horrors are to be expected in a narrative of Siberian exile, they land with a shocking impact after the musings that come before.

In "The Payback," two young women develop a complex friendship as they master the art of felling trees. Their frustrations, their clashes of personality, their differences in perspective could have happened anywhere, but here their reliance on each other for basic survival forces them to forge an intimate relationship. They not only share their dreams but also hurt one another deeply.

Mash portrays life in the postwar Moldavian Soviet Socialist Republic as a time of rebuilding, of searching for solace in an orphaned atmosphere. In "Mona Bubbe," she notes that Jews returning from evacuation were "hungry for something familiar" and cherished even the smallest reminders of their destroyed world, including the rantings of a man who is hauled off by the authorities for orating publicly in Hebrew. In this atmosphere of longing, Mona Bubbe, an old woman who listens devotedly to free concerts in the public park, finds a sense of validation in the idea that the orchestra depends on her admiration. As the musicians begin to emigrate, she feels abandoned. Once again she has lost her hold on the small rituals of daily life that hold her world together. In "The Irony of Fate," Mash reveals the nimble footwork required to navigate Israeli and Soviet bureaucracies. Time and again, her characters must adapt to sweeping social and political changes that profoundly alter their daily lives.

In writing about Israel, Mash provides a counter-narrative to the rosy idea of Israel as a place for the "natural" and rapid absorption of immigrants united by the bond of Jewishness. Instead, she depicts the disillusionment and unease that immigrants experience as they remember their homelands and struggle to find their footing in a new environment. In the longest piece in this volume, the story titled "Retirees," four Eastern European immigrants in the Israeli city of Ashdod are styled as the four sons who ask questions in the Haggadah, the text read during the feast of Passover. By turns argumentative and tender, they spend their days sitting together on a park bench telling their life stories. Their combative friendship helps them to adjust to new circumstances. In "Erika," the narrator finds a sense of mission as a Yiddish writer. Even though her audience is shrinking, she believes absolutely in the value and valor of her native tongue.

The stories in this collection are often subtle and at times witty and sardonic. The pacing of the narration follows the unfolding of the events themselves. In "The Bridegroom Tree," Mash lays before the reader with abundant clarity the fact that her town met with tragic destruction. Yet the meandering expository opening allows the final revelation to hit with the suddenness of the exploding bomb that the author describes. Likewise, in "Resting Place," the story at first drifts like the barge that carries the deportees; the climax of the story, with its concluding words about women performing burial rituals traditionally designated for men, arrives as an exhausted endpoint to the arduous journey. In "On the Landing," the delicate account tiptoes as carefully as Ester herself during her escape from the gulag, afraid to breathe as she reaches toward a discarded cookie. "Ingathering of Exiles" chatters along noisily, but ends abruptly with a whiff of the abyss—a chilling reminder of the dark truths carried by Mash's protagonists and by the lands in which they find themselves.

Born of a lifetime of repeated uprooting, Mash's literary oeuvre is a brave, resilient achievement that asserts the value of humanity itself. Her writing is imaginative, poignant, and relentlessly honest. Her stories remain urgently relevant in our moment as displaced people seek refuge across the globe. It is a joy to share them with new audiences.

Translator's Note

By Ellen Cassedy

Yiddish is what linguists call a "fusion language"—a Germanic tongue written in the Hebrew alphabet, with liberal helpings of Hebrew, Aramaic, and Slavic words stirred into the pot. Over the centuries, the mix of linguistic elements has reflected the lives of Yiddish speakers themselves—lives in which people from diverse cultures rub elbows, political boundaries are always shifting, and "home" is an elusive concept. For many Eastern European Jews and their descendants throughout the world, the language has functioned as a portable homeland, a touchstone.

Yenta Mash's Yiddish is alive with regionalisms carried to new places, bits and pieces of multiple languages picked up along the way, and neologisms invented to describe new circumstances. Given the shifting eras, regimes, and linguistic contexts, I've sometimes deviated from the standard transliteration system for Yiddish established by YIVO, the institute for Jewish research based in New York. The intermingling of cultures in the Soviet Union is reflected in the Yiddish spelling of some Russian-style names (e.g., Avrom Grigorievitsh). And in stories set in Israel, I sometimes have Mash's characters choose the European pronunciation for certain words and other times opt for the Israeli pronunciation. In "The Second Time Around," for example, Ella uses the word "Shabbos," in the Yiddish style, when talking about the Sabbath. But in "Ingathering of Exiles," when the narrator (also an Eastern European Jew) tells us that shops are officially closed on the day of rest, I have her say "Shabbat," in the Israeli style.

I've spelled place names in such a way that readers can find them on a map. A town known to Yiddish speakers as Belz, for example, appears here as Bălți, as it's officially spelled in present-day Moldova. An exception is Kishinev (Chişinău on the map), which, unlike most Moldovan cities, is known to many English-language readers in its Yiddish version.

Amy Farranto and her colleagues at Northern Illinois University Press were a pleasure to work with. I'm grateful to Jessica Kirzane for her insights and her generous collaborative spirit, and to Regina Novak and to Daniel Galay of H. Leyvik Publishing House for permission to translate Mash's stories.

I thank the Yiddish Book Center for its support and am grateful to have received a PEN/Heim Translation Fund Grant and a research fellowship from the Hadassah Brandeis Institute for work on this volume.

In Yiddish, *di goldene keyt,* the golden chain, refers to the Jewish literary tradition as it is passed down from one generation to the next. It is an honor to be able to add a link to the chain.